Osbourne

The Instruments of Jehann

Isaiah Burt

AN IMPRINT OF CONCEPT MOON STUDIOS INC.

Copyright © 2024 by Concept Moon Studios

All rights reserved. No part of this publication may be reproduced, distributed, or transmitted in any form or by any means, including photocopying, recording, or other electronic or mechanical methods, without the prior written permission of the publisher, except in the case of brief quotations embodied in critical reviews and certain other noncommercial uses permitted by copyright law.

This is a work of fiction. Names, characters, places, and incidents either are the product of the author's imagination or are used fictitiously. Any resemblance to actual persons, living or dead, events, or locales is entirely coincidental.

NO AI TRAINING: Without in any way limiting the author's [and publisher's] exclusive rights under copyright, any use of this publication to "train" generative artificial intelligence (AI) technologies to generate text is expressly prohibited. The author reserves all rights to license uses of this work for generative AI training and development of machine learning language models.

The Instruments of Jehann created by B.D. Didley

Cover Design by La'Vata O'Neal

Cover Text and Back Cover Art by Anastasia Ruth

Inside Cover Page Axe by Morgan Burt

Chapter Art Crossed Axes by Dean Spencer

Author Photo by Tammy Lese

ISBN 979-8-3426495-8-2

Published by Concept Moon Studios

www.conceptmoon.com

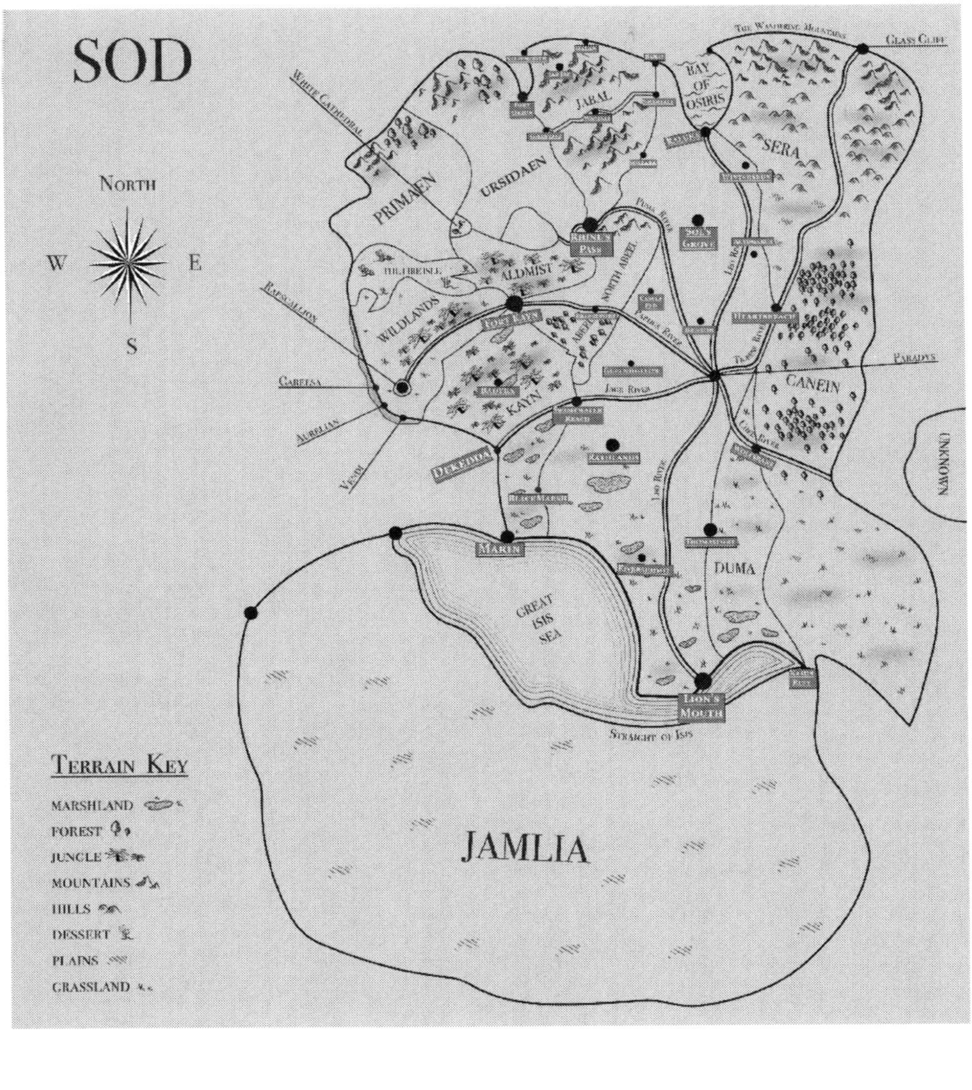
SOD
NORTH
W
E
S
THE WANDERING MOUNTAINS
GLASS CLIFF
WHITE CATHEDRAL
BAY OF OSIRIS
JABAL
SERA
PRIMAEN
URSIDAEN
ALDMIST
WILDLANDS
NORTH ABYEL
RHINE'S PASS
KAYN
CANEIN
PARADYS
RAFSCALLION
CABETSA
AURELIAN
VENDI
UNKNOWN
MARIS
GREAT ISIS SEA
DUMA
LION'S MOUTH
STRAIGHT OF ISIS
JAMLIA
TERRAIN KEY
MARSHLAND
FOREST
JUNGLE
MOUNTAINS
HILLS
DESSERT
PLAINS
GRASSLAND

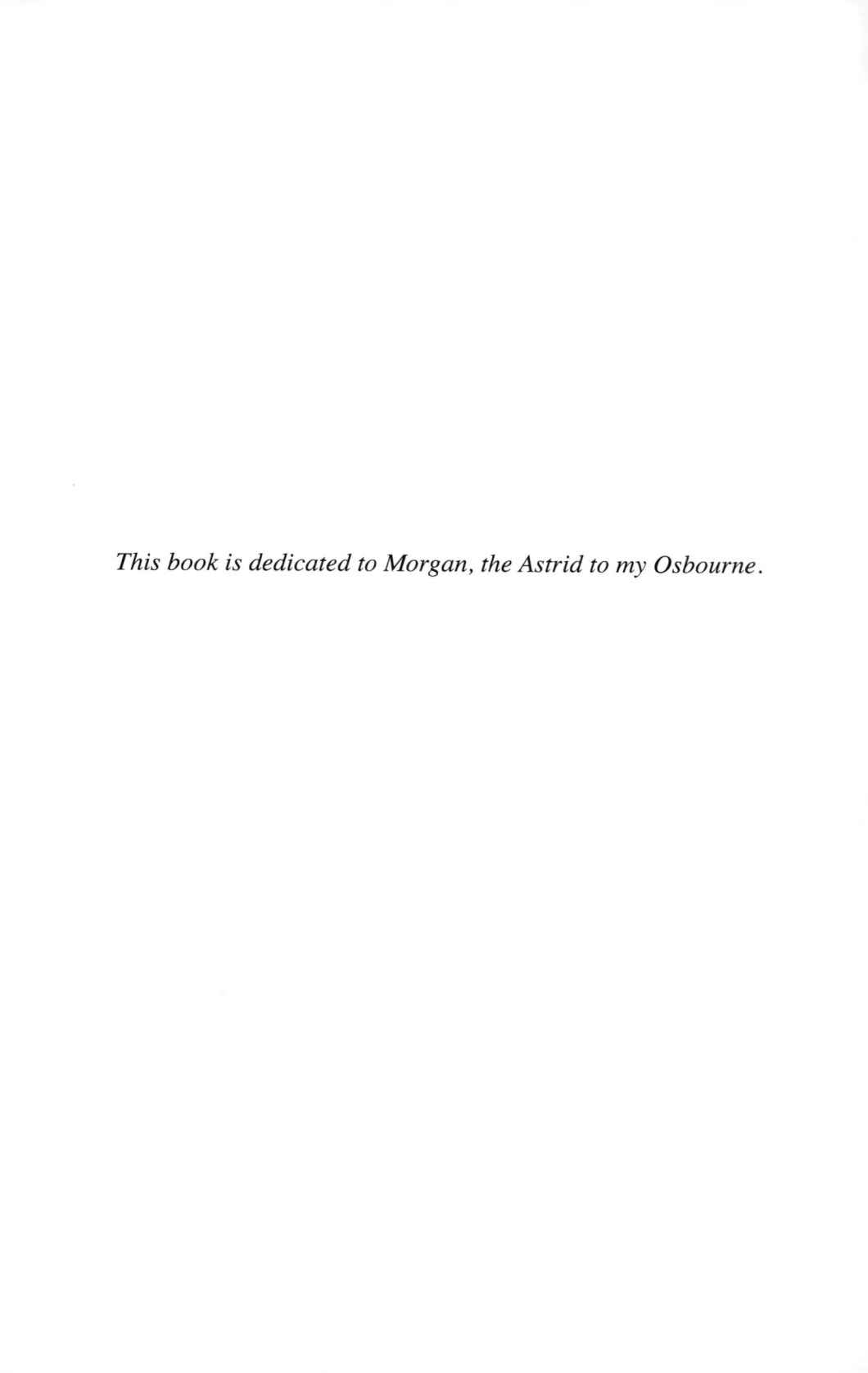

This book is dedicated to Morgan, the Astrid to my Osbourne.

Contents

Foreword

Dramatis Personae

Part I: Encroachment

    1

    2

    3

    4

    5

    6

    7

    8

Part II: Heart of Darkness

    9

    10

    11

    12

    13

    14

    15

Glossary

    About the Author

Foreword

From the time I finished the first full draft of Osbourne, I knew that the day would come when the book would finally be published. Eventually. But, as any published author will tell you, knowing that the day will come and experiencing it when it does are two entirely different matters.

Osbourne has been a journey in every sense of the word. It is so much more than the short story it started as three years ago, and I have learned more about myself as a person and as a writer throughout the process of expanding, revising, and rewriting it. Move aside, Diabolical Ascension; my new magnum opus has arrived!

I jest, of course. I could never leave Zeraga Baal'khal behind, but that is a matter of another foreword yet to be written. Stay vigilant, my fanatics.

My journey with Concept Moon Studios started shortly before the writing of Osbourne began. B.D. was looking for writers to work on his Instruments of Jehann project, and the spectacular art he was advertising with got me to check it out. I reached out, we exchanged material, and we negotiated. Soon enough, a bargain was struck; a contract was signed. The pact was sealed. This has since proven to be one of my best decisions.

One of the first things B.D. said when our freshly assembled writing team started was that Jehann could be anything. He has more than delivered on that. He's made space to hear me every time I have a new idea, and he's supported my work every step of the way, Concept Moon and otherwise. It is because of Instruments that I've had the opportunity to be part of something much bigger than myself, but more than that, Instruments feels like home. Thank you, B.D. I am so glad we met, brother. You have my utmost admiration and respect.

Now for the rest of you! Cassandra, thank you for helping me work out the general details of Ursidaen culture. Alana, thank you for reading the first draft of Osbourne and being both gentle and uncompromising in your feedback. Seeing how far Osbourne has come has given me more appreciation of that, and it has helped me become a better writer. Michelle, thank you for reading and giving me feedback on drafts; finding our beta reader; and spearheading our marketing efforts. La'Vata, your work on the cover absolutely blew me away. You manifested Osbourne as he is meant to be. Thank you. Everett, I enjoy the camaraderie we share as dark fantasy writers and tabletop gamers, and it makes me smile when you get my obscure heavy metal references. Jessica, thank you for your unconditional support of myself and everyone else on the team.

During the writing of Osbourne, I went through some big changes in my life. Most related are the relationships I've built with other publishers. Through these, I gained confidence and pushed myself to keep developing my craft. My successes in these other writing arenas inspired me to come back to Osbourne with greater fervor. In particular, I'd like to thank four individuals who have been radically influential on my writing journey: Daniel Davis, Neal Litherland, Adrian Kennelly, and Tyler Thompson. Thank you all for your support, your advice, and believing in me.

Another change that happened was the passing of my mother. I wish that she was here to read what I have written and to know that her son has done what he set out to do. When I told B.D. and the rest of the Instruments team about this, the amount of unconditional support and understanding I received was humbling. I wasn't just a fellow writer. I was a friend. I'll never forget that.

The Instruments team also supported me through an even bigger, much more positive change, too: getting married to my beautiful, intelligent, humorous, and unendingly devoted wife, Morgan. We met and bonded over a shared love of fantasy fiction, and it was through our own collaborative project that I received my first real kick in the arse to improve my craft from someone who cared. Since then, we have built a wonderful life together filled with love, happiness, and more projects than we know what to do with. Thank you, Morgan. You are my best friend, my partner, my everything. No matter what comes my way, you're always there to help find the solution that works best for us, and you're always trying to help me (even if that looks like another kick in the arse!). You've shown me what home should look like and feel like, and I am grateful for the compassion you show me when I make a mistake (or try to outsmart myself). You have a level head and a caring heart. You keep me moving in the right direction. You keep my life rich and colorful.

I love you.

With marriage came another strange thing: family. Morgan's parents, Diane and Dennis, gladly adopted me as their own son, and I am grateful for that now more than ever. Mom, I enjoy hearing you talk about your cooking, sewing, writing, and really anything else. Dad, you have been a font of earthly wisdom, a listening ear, and an eager teacher in the arcane workings of automobiles. And, it certainly doesn't hurt that both of you are as geeky as Morgan and I. I love you both.

And there you have it. It takes a village, right? To those who, in my humanness, I have forgotten to mention here but deserve my thanks: you know who you are. Thank you.

Now, my dear reader, turn the page and get ready to ride the lightning!

Dramatis Personae

Osbourne Gudbrandr- Polar bear berserker and skald of Clan Eldingblod. He also has the ability to channel lightning. He is known for his sense of justice, his commitment to his comrades, and his devotion to his wife.

Astrid Gudbrandr- Polar bear warrior of Clan Eldingblod. She is Osbourne's wife. She is soft-spoken but committed to her husband and clan. She is always working on improving her fighting skills.

Kolvar Bjornsson- Older grizzly bear who is one of the Odofrélsa (senior warriors; see glossary) of Clan Eldingblod. He commands the pack that the other bears are apart of and is known for being a noble, level-headed beast.

Bror Halvarson- Grizzly bear warrior-mage of Clan Eldingblod. He has the ability to channel fire, and he is known for being ambitious, cunning, and ruthless.

Hyddi Arvydr- Black bear warrior-mage of Clan Eldingblod. Her magical powers grant her glimpses into the future. Among her pack, she is seen as a font of wisdom, always considering the consequences before acting.

Olaf Ebbenberg- Grizzly bear berserker of Clan Eldingblod. He is known for his confidence and his willingness to make his opinions known no matter what, but he will do anything to help his comrades.

Váli Fryg- Black bear berserker of Clan Eldingblod. Few understand the terrible wrath of the berserkers better than him; he calls upon his power only when necessary. He is deeply devoted to his family.

Kjevvi Gudbrandr- Now deceased, Kjevvi was a polar bear berserker and lightning wielder of Clan Eldingblod, and he is Osbourne's father. It is from Kjevvi that Osbourne learned about his powers.

Ingrid Gudbrandr- Now deceased, Ingrid was a polar bear warrior of Clan Eldingblod, and she is Osbourne's mother.

Bodil Vjarnen- A venerable black bear oracle whose clan and lineage are unknown. She guides Osbourne on his quest.

Xihhsil- A naga shaman from one of the tribes on the border of Ursidaen and Aldmist. He wields the power of light and proves to be Osbourne's unlikeliest ally.

Part I: Encroachment

1

The two polar bears circled each other, their armor clinking and their weapons brandished.

"Afraid to strike first, Ozzy?" the Ursidaen she-beast said with a snicker. She was the only one he permitted to call him that, a nickname from when they were cubs.

"You should know better than to be begging for me to strike first, Astrid." Osbourne flexed his grip on his axe. Truth be told, he was glad at how well he had hidden his slight start at Astrid's words. He had become so lost in admiring *her* that he had forgotten they were supposed to be sparring. Even after five years of marriage, there was nothing that made Osbourne's heart melt the way Astrid's gaze did. Her cerulean eyes sparkled in the rising midmorning light and gleamed with fierce determination.

Astrid grinned. "Really, Ozzy? Nothing?"

"If you are so eager to lose, then strike the first blow." Osbourne punctuated his statement by slamming the flat of his axe against his shield. Knowing when to initiate combat was just as important as knowing the techniques themselves, and Osbourne couldn't bring himself to swing first, not at his mate. He gritted his teeth as the geometric runes on his axe flashed with lightning, his Gift yearning for release.

"None of that sorcery of yours, remember?" There was a slight tremor in Astrid's voice.

"I know," Osbourne replied, "No berserking, no Gift, and none of my songs or calls." He said the words as much for himself as his mate, and he fought back a crimson ring about his vision as he tried to ignore the tingling, almost burning, sensation of lightning in his veins. His skaldic power was the easiest to control of the three, but even that could lend a burst of strength at an inopportune moment.

Lunging, Astrid drove her double-edged sword toward Osbourne, the weapon's filigreed hilt gleaming in the morning light while keeping her shield close to her chest.

Osbourne hid a nervous flash behind a wry smirk. She was so predictable. Being predictable on the battlefield got beasts killed, and they were due to be leaving as part of a scouting warband later that day. Osbourne blocked Astrid's sword before retaliating with a stroke of his axe, pulling the blow so that he wouldn't exploit the opening at his mate's waist. Astrid stepped back into a closed, bulwark-like position. Osbourne's axe harmlessly swished through the air in front of her.

"Your footwork has gotten better," Osbourne said.

"So has your restraint," Astrid replied.

Osbourne chuckled and took a breath, trying not to sound too relieved as he exhaled. "Now, you will have to get good enough that I will not need it." The words were more accurate than he wanted them to be. Though he and his mate were both old enough to be considered full warriors of the nation of Ursidaen, Astrid had had to complete the trials three times before being accepted as such. Now, rumors abounded that the gorillas of nearby Primean were being more aggressive, even going so far as to enter Ursidaen itself.

Such an occurrence was far from uncommon. The nations of beasts which inhabited Sod were rarely on friendly terms with one another. Centuries ago, the lions of the Heartlands had marched forth to bring the whole continent under their rule, presumably intending to conquer the rest of Terran next. Though the lions had mostly succeeded in "unifying" Sod, as they put it, the other cat nations chafed under the weight of the lions' crown, and other countries had rejected the lions' offer of "peace" entirely: the bears of Ursidaen; the gorillas of Primean; the lizards of Aldmist; the wolves of Canein; and the elephants of Jamlia.

Still, the rumors of Primean encroachment were troubling since autumn was fast yielding to winter. Osbourne and Astrid were part of the pack, a few dozen bears strong, sent to patrol the region around their hometown of Havaeborg and find out if the rumors were true. Osbourne hoped that they were not. The leadership of his clan, Clan Eldingblod, had not wanted to take any chances. A Primean raid on Havaeborg had killed many good bears, Osbourne's parents among them. That was why he wielded his father's axe. It was also why he had been chosen for this pack. Astrid, however, had been chosen despite Osbourne's protests. Battle with the Primeans seemed inevitable, and it was likely that the chaos would separate him from *her*, his mate, his best friend, and his last link to his parents.

"Getting lost in yourself again, Ozzy?" Astrid said, interrupting his thoughts. "I could have struck three times during that pause. Don't tell me you're getting too slow to fight already."

"Careful now," Osbourne rumbled. He punctuated his statement with a brutal, cleaving stroke of his axe. As its edge tore through the air, his muscles tensed from the Gift still burning in his veins, clawing to be set free.

Astrid dodged, and she used the motion to propel herself forward, ramming her shield into Osbourne and sending him staggering back. Pressing her advantage, Astrid struck at Osbourne's shoulder with her sword.

The blow was too close for him to dodge; his greater size and bulk worked against him. Astrid's sword slammed into his armor, and the ringing of steel echoed across the damp grass. Osbourne's chest throbbed, but no blood flowed.

"Yes, you're definitely slowing down," Astrid laughed.

"You know that I was never quick to begin with, but—" Osbourne slammed his shield into Astrid's gut, tearing the breath from her lungs and sending her staggering back. "It's all about precision and strength." The polar bear stepped back into a defensive stance so that his mate had the time and space to recover herself.

Astrid assumed a stance with her body at an angle, placing her shield forward and her sword just behind. "You're going easy on me, Osbourne."

"That is the point, is it not?" the other polar bear replied coolly.

Though anyone else would have thought that Astrid was ready to keep fighting, Osbourne knew better. His mate's stance had loosened, creating an opening between her sword and shield, and her ears were laid back rather than perked up. Already, her eyes were starting to swirl with weariness.

Osbourne glanced up at the sky. The rose pink of the morning was fading to pale blue. The world trees had finished lavishing the land with the first bout of daylight. Collectively known as Sha-Jara, one stood at the very top of the world while the other was rooted at the bottom. From them was said to come all life.

Lowering his weapons, Osbourne said, "Perhaps we should stop for today." He was loathe to admit it, but he barely kept himself from panting, winded from the exertion, and his muscles pulsed with hot pain. Even the burning of the Gift had dulled without his energy to keep feeding it, and the crimson about his vision had disappeared. He had not gone as easy as Astrid wanted to believe, but he was proud of her because of it.

"Come on, Ozzy," Astrid whined, "We still have at least another hour before we have to go back."

Osbourne caught the undertone of desperation in her voice. It was a conflict that Osbourne and all other bears knew well. Ursidaens hated to admit when they could no longer fight, even in training bouts.

"Alright now," Osbourne said, "I will make you a deal: we can go for one more bout, but only if you strike first."

"Then we'll make it a good one, Ozzy." Astrid gave a dazzling smile that Osbourne couldn't help but return. In the next moment, Astrid threw herself at Osbourne, abandoning all pretenses of defense; her only goal was to strike and strike hard.

Osbourne parried Astrid's first strike with his axe before blocking the second one with his shield. The third strike came from above, forcing Osbourne to pivot out of the way. He had little doubt that the blow would have split his skull open if he had remained still.

"Yes!" Osbourne cried as he raised his shield. "More!" New vigor seeped into the polar bear's weary flesh, a skaldic call he had not intended to make.

Astrid seemed not to notice; strike after strike rained down upon Osbourne's shield, sending shock and pain coursing up his shoulder.

As the next strike came down upon Osbourne, he beat Astrid's sword back with his axe before slamming her with his shield. Astrid did not yield a single step.

"Good! Good!" Osbourne said as he swung again. His heart skipped a beat as he realized he had aimed for Astrid's neck. Crimson ringed his vision, and the berserker rage gnawed at him now that blood was but a breath away.

Astrid narrowly parried; the rasp of steel against steel was music to ears that were now perked up.

Osbourne's face settled into stoicism as he swung again, this time opting for the kind of overwhelmingly strong overhead chop that the berserkers were known for. Astrid threw her shield up to block, but Osbourne's axe tore through it and the ringmail underneath to graze his mate's forearm. A trickle of blood followed, bringing a pang of guilt that was soon buried. The crimson at the edges of Osbourne's vision thickened; the rage was now a sharp ticking in his mind; his flesh begged for him to give in.

With a deep breath, Osbourne pushed back the vicious urges. "The duel is done." He lowered his axe and stepped back.

"Yes," Astrid agreed as she locked gazes with her mate. "Thank you, Ozzy."

Osbourne's face softened at the unfettered admiration in her eyes. They sheathed their weapons, embraced one another, and shared a kiss.

"I hope that cut does not hurt too much," Osbourne said, trying not to think about what would have happened if his strike had hit a little harder or landed a little higher... A knot formed in his chest.

"Pain is how we learn." Astrid was smiling.

"Spoken like a true Odolig." It was the ancient word for warrior, and Astrid had definitely earned the title this morning.

Astrid pressed her face into Osbourne's neck and held him tighter, sighing contentedly. She was home.

"I suppose we should return to camp now," Astrid said as she finally pulled away.

"Finenr is not going to like what happened to your shield," Osbourne replied before taking a moment to examine the splintered wood. "I did quite a number on it."

"He grumbles no matter how small the fix is, and Bror will no doubt be looking for us soon."

"Aye. We both know how that bear is." Osbourne frowned. Bror was one of the higher-ranking warriors responsible for leading warbands within a pack, and as far as Osbourne was concerned, Bror enjoyed the position too much.

Osbourne and Astrid set a quick pace across the flat ground. A pair of banners depicting the crossed lightning bolts and roaring bear heads of Clan Eldingblod appeared on the horizon, followed by tents of dunatar skin and reinforced canvas. Between them were rock rings containing cooking fires now reduced to embers. Armed and armored bears went about their duties.

"I'm going to find Finenr," Astrid said, "With any luck, I can get my shield repaired before we have to meet Bror."

"Aye." Osbourne nodded, and his stomach growled. "I am going to see if there are any leftovers from breakfast." Holding back his powers during sparring had taken more out of him than he had expected.

The polar bears kissed, savoring the blissful moment. Osbourne's gaze lingered on Astrid as they parted ways. She walked with grace and confidence, completely in control of her movements and holding her head high, just as she had on the day she had finally earned her Odolig title. Letting out a sigh, Osbourne turned away, but in the back of his mind, fear gnawed at him.

2

The polar bears reunited half an hour later, Osbourne with his hunger satisfied and Astrid with her shield repaired.

"Look, Ozzy," Astrid said, "I'll have to wait to paint the new pieces until we get back home. But, other than that, it's good as new."

It was easy to see which boards of the rectangular shield had been replaced. Both the field of blue and Akksardi's scroll, the symbol of the god of wisdom, knowledge, and justice, were fragmented. But, the shield was functional. That was what mattered. Osbourne knew all too well that he would not always be there to protect Astrid. A year ago, he had unleashed a lightning storm during a raid and blacked out for a week. Astrid had never left his side. Since then, he never forgot that such a thing could happen again. He knew, as all berserkers knew, that he did not have long to live, more so because the Gift burned within him. Mortal flesh could only contain such power for so long. Osbourne's only hope was that he did not leave Astrid behind before they had a cub together. Kjevvi, after Osbourne's father, would be the cub's name if they had a boy, and they had chosen the name Erika, after Astrid's mother, for a girl.

"Is everything alright, Ozzy?" Astrid's voice was tinged with concern. "You're making that face again."

"I am fine," Osbourne replied, "Just thinking, nothing more."

"Care to tell me what?"

Osbourne gestured dismissively with his paw. "Nothing important."

Before Astrid could press the matter further, the deep, gravelly voice of an elderly Ursidaen male said, "Hail, Osbourne and Astrid." Both polar bears' ears perked up. A grizzly bear now stood before them, his face noble and etched with age, his immaculate battle-plate gleaming in the daylight. A crossed horn and axe were emblazoned upon his right pauldron, rendered in scintillating bronze, the symbol of the Odofrélsa.

"Kolvar," Osbourne replied, immediately recognizing the leader of his pack. "Is there something we can help you with?"

"Aye," Kolvar said, "Since you both will be working under Bror, I want you to keep an eye on him. He's set his sights on commanding a whole Hafna, and I want to make sure that he is up to the task before he goes to Rök to be judged by the Chieftain and Stone Carver."

"He always was an ambitious one," Osbourne said dryly, not liking the idea of Bror commanding three hundred bears. Kolvar had more than earned that honor through blood, sweat, and long, sleepless nights. Bror, however… That grizzly bear was a skilled warrior and tactician, but his Gift for conjuring flames matched his personality too well.

Astrid said nothing as she nodded her agreement.

"That he is," Kolvar said, "Thank you, Osbourne. Thank you, Astrid." He turned around and walked away.

"Lucky us," Astrid said once Kolvar was out of ear shot.

"Yes," Osbourne replied, "lucky us." He knew that Kolvar had not chosen him to lead the warband on the simple fact that he would refuse. Osbourne was a skilled warrior, and the camaraderie he shared with his fellows was equaled by few. But with how much effort it took to control his berserker rage, and his Gift of lightning on top of that? He had never felt that he would be able to give the task of leadership the attention it deserved.

Now, he wondered if that mindset would prove too timorous.

3

Every other bear in the camp was up and ready. Three days of harsh marching and talk of what would come next had permeated the warband with a sharp discipline born from muscle memory and looming uncertainty. They all had done these procedures dozens of times, and no beast was taking any chances. Osbourne and Astrid were the last to arrive.

"I hope Kraan's warmth has found you this morning," Bror said to them.

"It has, which I am glad for. The first snows of winter are coming soon. I can smell it in the air." Osbourne was melancholic at the sight of all the steel around him. Such bears were indeed a formidable sight, but it was all but assured that some of them would not come back.

"Good." Bror gave a curt nod. "I would like for you to lead the other berserkers into battle against the Primeans."

"They have been found already?" An undertone of skepticism lurked in Osbourne's voice. There was still a decent distance between the warband and the Ursidaen-Primean border.

Bror nodded. "Hyddi saw them in her divinations an hour ago." He gestured toward a black bear. She, like Bror, was a warrior-mage, though her Gift allowed her to glimpse the future. "The *apes'* camp is only ten miles east of here. I want you and the other berserkers to lay waste to it."

"With all due respect, Trynjul, are you sure that is the wisest course of action?" Osbourne kept himself from gritting his teeth as he addressed Bror by his rank in the ancient tongue. He didn't feel that the other bear deserved it, but it was the best way to get him to listen. If the rumors of Primean encroachment proved true, open war would surely follow.

Bror's face hardened. "Is there something you wish to say, Usyling Osbourne?"

"Would it not be beneficial to find out why they are here?"

"We need not waste time on that which is already known. They're only bloodthirsty *apes*, after all."

"The Primeans will have their opportunity for bloodshed soon when the next Culling happens," Osbourne reasoned. The Culling was a grand tournament held every twenty-five years for the dual purpose of settling political disputes and letting out bad blood in order to keep relative peace between the raiding nations. "Do you really believe that bloodthirst is the only reason the Primeans have delved so deep into our country?"

"It is the only thing the *apes* know. We both fought them at the last Culling and saw which of them became Thanes and which of them died."

"And what if they surrender to us? As leader of this warband, I assume that you have a plan for that."

"You have already asked your question, Osbourne." Bror straightened his shoulders as his chest rose. "Besides, a warrior such as yourself should have no issue deciding what needs to be done."

Osbourne remained still. His gaze was narrow; his words were calm. "A warrior such as myself consults his leaders before taking action." He paused. "If you do not answer me now, you will still have to answer before the pack."

As if on cue, the other bears exchanged uncertain looks and whispered words. Tension thickened in the air as Bror fell into a pensive silence.

"Use your own discretion," the grizzly bear finally said, his voice laced with an undertone of frustration despite his apathetic facial expression.

"Very well."

Osbourne threw a glance over his shoulder and saw Olaf and Váli, the other berserkers in the warband, coming forward. The grizzly bear and the black bear walked with their heads held high, their gazes swiveling about the gathered beasts, their armor rattling with every step. Each one held an enormous axe, more than twice the size of Osbourne's own, that was the signature weapon of the berserker caste.

"Tordok's vigor fill you, brothers." Osbourne walked toward them. "Bror has just given us our first task."

"Oh?" Váli asked.

"He said that a Primean camp has been spotted." Osbourne paused. "He wants us to lay waste to it."

Váli glanced at Bror, then back at Osbourne. "How big is the camp?"

"He did not say. He does not expect there to be any survivors."

"Of course, he doesn't." Olaf snorted derisively. "He's always thought of us berserkers as being mere butchers." He turned and stepped toward Bror. "Isn't that right, Bror? We are just killers."

Osbourne grinned. One thing he respected most about other berserkers was how willingly and fearlessly they spoke out against leaders who had become too haughty for their own good.

"The berserkers are mighty warriors," Bror said carefully. "That is why they have the reputation that they do. It is because of that that I wanted to send the three of you to execute the initial strike against the Primeans. We will end this before it begins."

"Hopefully." Váli turned to join Olaf. The berserkers stepped toward Bror, darkening him in their shadows. "It is just as likely that we will provoke them to great wrath. They would jump on the idea of avenging their fallen brethren. Are you willing to be responsible for starting a war?"

"War is our way of life." Bror crossed his arms. "Beasts fight. Beasts die. Those who live grow stronger."

"While that is true," Olaf said, "would it not be better to send scouts to investigate the camp first and find out what exactly we are up against? As I recall, Kolvar assigned three warriors who are skilled at tracking to this warband for that exact purpose."

Bror tilted his chin up, his eyes narrowing at the mention of the higher-ranking warrior. "Do you mean to say that you lack confidence in your fighting skill and that of the other Usyling?"

"No, merely that this mission should be executed with more finesse." Olaf's voice lowered into a growl.

Bror's expression darkened. "I never thought I would see the day when berserkers went soft."

Do you have any loved ones back in Havaeborg?" Váli said, letting the question hang in the air.

Osbourne looked at Olaf, who remained silent. Osbourne knew why: the grizzly bear fought so his mate and cubs would not have to.

"I do," Váli continued, "I have a husband. We adopted a cub together, one whose parents died during last year's raiding season. I would like to live to return to them instead of charging blindly into what could be a suicide mission."

"Then you should never have become a berserker," Bror replied, "However, I do thank you for admitting your liability. You will stay back at camp on latrine duty."

"Really now?" Váli was bristling. "You hear that, Osbourne? Having a family makes me a liability."

Astrid's face, her shining eyes, and her dazzling smile surged to the front of Osbourne's mind. The polar bear scowled at Bror. "Is this what you wanted? Not only have you insulted your clan-beasts, but now there are only two of us going on this ill-planned attack."

Bror shrugged. "They are mere *apes* against mighty berserkers, one of whom is a skald who can command lightning. I am sure that this task is within your and Olaf's ability to handle."

Osbourne's gaze hardened. He wanted nothing more than to throw Bror to the ground and wipe the condescension off his face. "It is never wise to underestimate a foe."

"You're certainly right, Usyling Osbourne, and so it is a good thing that I am not known for miscalculating." Bror glanced between the two berserkers. "You both are to head eastward as soon as you are able. We cannot allow the Primeans to remain in our country."

Both berserkers nodded, at which point Bror dismissed them with a wave of his paw.

Astrid rushed over to Osbourne, her blue eyes bright with worry. "Be safe, my love."

"I will." Osbourne brought his paw up to his mate's face and kissed her. "I will." It was all he could say. Refusing to go would mean dishonor, but now he confronted the very real possibility that he would be outmatched.

One stray axe stroke, one wrong step, could seal his fate at the best of times. He tried not to think of the sight of Astrid weeping at his grave.

4

Osbourne hated to admit it, but Bror's intelligence had been right. The Primean camp was close, much closer than he had expected. Out of all the nations on Sod, there were only two whose main residents didn't walk on paws: the elephants of Jamlia and the gorillas of Primean. And the tracks that Osbourne and Olaf followed definitely hadn't been left by elephants. More so, the scents of dung and urine, nearly rancid, lingered in the air. Osbourne scrunched his nose.

The sights and smells troubled Osbourne, but they were too blatant to be denied. The Primeans might as well have declared war. And with the gorilla nation's larger armies and unscrupulous tactics… Osbourne clenched his paws. Astrid had never gone on a raid before, let alone seen a pitched battle. If any gorilla so much as touched her, Osbourne knew that he would gladly kill every last one of them. Anything to protect *her*.

"I smell it, too." Olaf flexed his grip on his axe. The freshly sharpened blade gleamed in the daylight. "If that is anything to go by, there's definitely more of them than us."

"Aye," Osbourne replied, "I wish that Váli were here."

"Me too."

The two bears went forward a few more strides. The outlines of tents became visible.

"There it is." Osbourne pulled his axe from his belt and unshouldered his shield.

"Aye." Olaf nodded. "Looks like it's time to go prove Bror right." The grizzly bear's words were thick with grim humor.

"The only problem is that there are not any Primeans around." Osbourne's voice was just as grim as his companion's, but it had none of the humor. With how loud the warband had been during the last three days of marching, Osbourne would not have been surprised to learn that the gorillas had prepared an ambush. That was what he would have done, and he had to concede that it was likely what Bror would have done, too. The thought of Bror lying in wait to unleash an inferno and watch as every beast crumbled to ashes sent a shudder down Osbourne's spine.

Osbourne's ears perked up at a whistling sound from his left. A moment later, a Primean spear punched through his armor, burying itself in his flesh. He roared in agony as hot blood gushed from the wound. He did not have to look far to see the source of the attack; a Primean chariot barreled toward him across a thin field of freshly fallen snow that was already stained crimson.

The brutish iron vehicle bristled with spikes and was pulled by a gorilla twice as large as Osbourne. The gorilla's muscles and veins bulged through his skin, and his formerly sleek hair had fallen out in considerable chunks. Unfettered bloodlust was plastered to his face while his eyes were red with deathly hunger. No words came from the blood-beast's slavering jaws, only a guttural howl. Such were the results of the combat drugs that were part and parcel of Primean culture, another tool to win at any cost.

Osbourne heard Olaf clack his teeth and snarl as he charged straight toward his foes. He closed the distance quickly, letting out another roar as he brought his mighty axe down upon the blood-beast. Even though the giant gorilla was weighed down by the reins of the chariot, he still managed to lash out at Olaf with a fist. Having already committed to his attack, Olaf could not dodge; the blood-beast's fist slammed into him and sent him staggering back.

Osbourne roared as his vision turned red, his rage begging for righteous retribution. The polar bear tore the spear from his shoulder and hurled it back at the Primean as he launched himself into a run. The pain in his shoulder became nothing more than a dull thud that could be attended to later.

The Primean who drove the chariot dodged Osbourne's spear as he drew his sword and cleaved at Olaf. Letting out a snarl, Olaf blocked the blade and pushed it back toward his foe, metal grinding against metal. Osbourne's axe whistled as it hurtled toward the blood-beast. The giant gorilla tried to dodge but became entangled in his reins; Osbourne's axe buried itself deep in the blood-beast's side. A loud crunch and a spray of gore followed. Another strike from Osbourne slew the blood-beast.

"Tordok's vigor fills my body!" Osbourne roared, "Tordok's lightning lend me its wrath!" He raised his axe to the sky, and both his skaldic power and the burning of the Gift filled him as the head of his weapon became wreathed in crackling lightning.

Osbourne let out another snarl as he hacked at his foe with his now-radiant weapon. The Primean scrambled from his chariot and threw up his shield, a rectangular slab of wood bound in iron. Osbourne's axe buried itself deep in the shield, sending splinters and sparks spraying forth. Osbourne tore his weapon free as he was rejoined by Olaf, allowing both berserkers to strike at their Primean foe in unison.

Knowing that his scale mail and shield could not save him, the Primean fled toward a nearby cluster of trees from which three more Primeans emerged. The four gorillas charged, and Osbourne gave a booming roar that shredded the air. From the wordless skaldic call came a fresh wave of vigor. He and Olaf charged to meet the Primeans head-on.

A hammer-wielding Primean swung at Olaf. What the gorilla had in power, he lost in finesse; Olaf sidestepped the blow and retaliated with a cleaving blow of his axe. The Primean blocked with his hammer, and the sound of ringing steel reverberated through the air.

Osbourne continued his pursuit of the original foe, hacking at the Primean once more with his axe. Though the lightning about its head had dulled, it endured by the strength of Osbourne's will. The Primean parried Osbourne's axe with his sword as an axe-wielding gorilla leaped into the fray, swinging both of his weapons at Osbourne. He blocked one with his shield and shifted so that the other struck his breastplate rather than his axe arm. The force of both blows sent Osbourne staggering back, but neither of the Primean's axes tasted his flesh.

"From the side!" Olaf roared.

Osbourne threw a glance over his shoulder. The last Primean was charging right at him, his greatsword raised. Flailing his shield at the axe-wielding Primean as a distraction, Osbourne darted back into a crouched defensive stance that turned him into a bulwark of steel, leather, and wood. The other gorilla's sword whistled through the air as he brought it down upon Osbourne. His rage was clawing and gnawing now, and the red around his vision thickened, demanding rather than begging. Osbourne sidestepped the sword-strike, grinning as the Primean's blade became planted in the ground, at which point the axe-wielding Primean threw himself at Osbourne, cleaving at him with both axes, one after another. Osbourne beat back one with his shield and parried the other with his axe.

Olaf's pain-filled roar overcame the crashing of steel against steel. Osbourne's ears perked up as he stole a glance through his peripheral vision. The grizzly bear berserker lay bleeding out, and the hammer-wielding Primean stood triumphantly over him. The original Primean slammed his sword against his shield as he gave a savage sneer.

Osbourne gave a roar born from a rage-filled heart as he lunged and cleaved at his foes with his axe. The axe-wielding Primean swung at Osbourne's axe with his own two, but the Ursidaen blocked with his shield. His axe continued on its path undeterred and cut deeply into the throat of the sword-wielding Primean, blood spraying from the wound as lightning raked across flesh. Osbourne roared again, triumphantly, and relished the hot, coppery-tasting droplets that landed on his tongue.

The polar bear locked gazes with the Primeans next to Olaf and charged, the clanging of his armor and stomping of his paws serving as his battle cry. Those Primeans answered the Ursidaen's charge while the axe-wielding gorilla came from behind. Osbourne ducked under a sword as he cleaved at the hammer-wielding Primean. Though the gorilla sidestepped, his swing at Osbourne missed. The Ursidaen then whirled around to face the axe-wielding Primean; both of the gorilla's weapons were already carving through the air.

Osbourne evaded them only because of how he threw himself into the third of his foes, the one wielding a sword and shield. The gorilla did not shy away, and Osbourne roared as his rage reared up with new strength. Vigor crashed through him as the red intensified; with it came a heightened sense of perception. It was as though a shroud had been lifted from his mind. He slammed his shield into the Primean before him, sending the gorilla staggering back, flowing into another block before parrying an axe with his own. A third roar erupted from Osbourne's mouth. As if on cue, more Primeans emerged from the surrounding foliage.

Osbourne hurled himself at Olaf and started to lift the wounded berserker. "Feel the pain," Osbourne growled in his companion's ear, imbuing his words with skaldic might, "and by doing so, live!"

Olaf reared up, reinvigorated by his companion's magic. He snatched up his axe with a roar and wasted no time in following Osbourne as he launched into a retreat back toward their warband's camp.

The Primeans gave chase, the axe-wielding one in the lead. Though he struggled to keep up with Osbourne and Olaf, he snapped his arm forward, throwing an axe. It whistled through the air as it soared toward Osbourne's skull.

"Down!" Olaf roared as he shoved Osbourne. The Primean's axe flew over the polar bear as his elbows hit the ground.

A wet, sickening crack followed, and Olaf cried out. Osbourne looked over just in time to see his companion fall to the ground. A Primean axe sprouted from his spine, gore flowing like the unfettered red waterfall that it was.

"No!" Osbourne cried, "Tordok, grant me—"

"It will not work, Osbourne." Olaf's voice was hoarse and wan, and his eyes were turning misty with death. "Please, take care of Tyra and the cubs for me."

Osbourne nodded as tears formed in his eyes, and then Olaf was dead. The Primeans charged.

Osbourne rose in a flash, roaring as a paroxysm of anger and grief and hate overtook him like a tsunami. Everything turned red as uncontrolled lightning bolts screamed forth to smite everything in sight and scorch the earth itself. Charging forward was so natural that Osbourne barely registered he was doing it.

He was the rage; the rage was him; the Primeans died. Only once his grisly work was done did Osbourne finally yield to exhaustion.

5

Even in his dreams, Osbourne was not free of the rage.
It howled.
It remembered.

A cacophony of thunderous roars and ringing, clashing steel oppressed the air, gripping the town of Havaeborg like a vice. Stout longhouses and stone monuments that had stood for centuries were up in flames, and bears and gorillas were locked in mortal combat. Quarter was neither offered nor accepted.

Osbourne's parents had ordered him to stay in the house. He was not yet Odolig. Still, they had made sure that he had put on his ringmail and had an axe and shield, just in case.

The young polar bear stood just outside the door now. He couldn't stay inside. Red faintly ringed his vision; his lightning, the Gift, needled through his veins. The need to do battle, to join his parents, sang in every fiber of his flesh. All that kept him from charging into the melee, roaring at the top of his lungs, was *her*.

Astrid stood next to Osbourne, similarly garbed in ringmail, her sword and shield shaking in her grasp. "I'm scared, Ozzy." Her eyes sparkled with tears.

The Gift reared up with greater ardor at the sound of Astrid's fear. Snarling tendrils of lightning started crawling across the head of Osbourne's axe. He took a deep breath, filling his lungs until they burned. A bark of pain from his father tore his next breath from his mouth. Osbourne's gaze darted in that direction.

"You got me good there, you bastards," Kjevvi Gudbrandr snarled, "Too bad you will not be able to finish the job!" Osbourne's father was large, even by the standards of polar bears, darkening the three surrounding Primeans in his shadow. Blood-weeping gashes scored his flesh, and many of the rings on his armor were broken. His axe was a silhouette amid the pillar of lightning cocooning it, bathing him and his surroundings in actinic blue light.

Kjevvi's shield darted up to block an attack. A sweep of his axe followed, the polar bear letting out a guttural roar as a gorilla head went flying, the stump of his neck a red geyser. Three more Primeans darted in to replace the fallen one.

Another pain-filled cry rose above the din of battle. Osbourne tore his gaze away from his father to where Ingrid, his mother, had been, now covered by a mob of Primeans, their weapons rising and falling. Osbourne lurched forward; Astrid pulled him back. "Please, Ozzy, don't leave me." Ingrid cried out again, the sound overtaken by the hoots and roars of the now-cheering Primeans.

"No!" Kjevvi's roar rose above the pandemonium. "Ingrid!" Limbs flew with every chop of his axe as he forced his way through the melee to where his wife was. She was lying motionless and bleeding from more than a dozen places.

Kjevvi roared again. "I'll kill you all! You hear me? Every last one of you! Your lives are mine!"

Time seemed to slow down as Osbourne watched lightning embrace the whole of his father's body, bolts screaming and howling in every direction as he became an avatar of primordial fury. Primeans died with every stroke of his axe as he surged across the battlefield, streaks of red mist, evaporated gore, appearing in the lightning. Bears and gorillas alike fled from Kjevvi.

A shudder ran down Osbourne's spine, his limbs growing weak as all desire to join the battle fled. He had no words for the brutality that the Primeans had inflicted on his mother. Her motionless body wouldn't stop bleeding. Her face was forever locked in agony. There was only bewilderment and horror and revulsion and—

Kjevvi roared again. Another Primean lay dead beneath his hind paws, and tendrils of red mist coiled about his lightning-wreathed body. Was the bear that Osbourne saw now the same one he called father, the gentle beast who had taught him how to hold an axe, build a fire, and learn from his failures when they got the better of him? Osbourne's throat went dry as he faced the cold, hard truth. He didn't know, but he wanted to say yes. More than anything else, he wanted to know that that raging, hate-filled bear was still his father.

Osbourne's jaw dropped as he watched his father cut down a gorilla and pause to savor the blood spraying into his open jaws.

Kjevvi had told his cub that he had these same powers: the berserker rage and the Gift of Tordok's lightning. Was this, then, the fate that awaited Osbourne? Was he doomed to become lost in the same rage he witnessed now?

The remaining Primeans turned and fled, their cries of battle and triumph now ones of terror, all semblance of organization gone. And Kjevvi lashed out with his lightning, more gorillas dying as they were struck down by the hammer of the gods.

"Kjevvi!" The call came from Haralda, the grizzly bear running toward Osbourne's father. "Kjevvi, it's over! The Primeans are gone!"

The only reply Kjevvi gave Haralda, one of his best friends of twenty years, was a bellow of inchoate rage and a slash of his howling axe. The blade slammed into Haralda's shoulder with a sickening crack, the wound jetting blood as she crumpled to the ground. Kjevvi's next blow pulped her skull, and the rage-lost bear roared again. "Ingrid, my love, I am coming for you!"

Kjevvi's lightning brightened. Then came a deafening boom that left Osbourne's ears ringing. In an instant, the lightning soared upward, a pillar reaching for the heavens, evanescing as it did so. Kjevvi collapsed. He didn't so much as stir. The rage and the Gift had taken his life as payment and granted his last desire.

"No!" Osbourne screamed, tearing free from Astrid's grip as he ran to his father, falling to his knees as he arrived.

Kjevvi's eyes were closed; his face was sanguine; his wounds were blackened, cauterized. His right paw still held his axe, the rune-etched blade now indolent.

"Father..." Osbourne whispered, his voice choked and hoarse as tears formed in his eyes. He couldn't stop them from falling. He didn't try to. He didn't want to. "Father..."

Osbourne started at the sensation of a paw resting lightly on his shoulder. "Oh, Ozzy, I'm so sorry." Astrid wrapped her arms around her betrothed and held him tight.

Osbourne wept louder. "If I had helped him, he would still be here."

Astrid didn't say anything. She only hugged him tighter.

Osbourne laid his paw on his father's, the one holding the axe, and wept for a while longer until his eyes were dry and his throat was ragged. Only then did he look up at Astrid.

"Thank you," he whispered.

"Of course, Ozzy." Astrid kissed his forehead. "I love you."

*   *   *

Osbourne jolted awake from the nightmare. He lay in an agglutination of cold sweat, crusted gore, and half-melted snow, and the chill night breeze caressed him with every pass. For a moment, Osbourne wondered where he was. He blinked his eyes and looked up. Three moons hung in the sky. Foremost among them was a full blue moon, the Warrior. To the east shone the Maiden, pale peach and half-full. The Child was but a sickle of yellow light to the west, dulled by the Warrior's luminescence. The blanketing light of that dominant moon made the snow seem almost like stone.

Osbourne's gaze drifted onto a nearby Primean corpse, the skull split open, and the brains spilled out, the scene made ghastlier by the unrelenting gloom all around. Everything came back to Osbourne like a hammer striking an anvil again and again and again; he relived the slaughter of the previous day compressed into the span of a mere moment. The gorillas were dead. And so was Olaf.

Osbourne rose to his hind paws and, after making sure he still had his own axe and shield, sought out Olaf's body. He soon found it.

The grizzly bear was a husk of who he had been in life, mired in his own gore, sweat, and excrement, his axe an arm's length away. Osbourne sighed and shook his head. He couldn't give Olaf a proper burial, not when more Primeans could arrive at any moment. It was a Tordok-granted miracle that more hadn't arrived already. But Osbourne couldn't leave his comrade like this. Pointing his axe, Kjevvi's axe, at Olaf's body, Osbourne called upon his Gift. An electric sensation flowed through his arm as his weapon started glowing, culminating in a lightning bolt that set Olaf's body aflame. The fire blossomed into radiance from the ample fuel all around.

"To Tordok's realm, you go, fellow Usyling," Osbourne whispered.

The polar bear watched in mournful silence until Olaf's body was no more. Affixing his now-dimmed axe to his belt, he knelt and picked up Olaf's axe, the mighty weapon of a mighty warrior. As Osbourne rose, movement flashed in his peripheral. His gaze snapped toward the source, a stirring gorilla.

Osbourne walked over to the Primean. She was as cut and ragged as he was. It was a miracle she was alive at all. Her emotionless gaze met Osbourne's.

"End it and leave, bear," she rasped.

"And why should I do that?" Osbourne replied.

"More are coming."

"Why?" Osbourne was nearly growling. "Why are your beasts invading Ursidaen? We have done nothing to provoke it."

"More land, more distance."

"More distance from what? Are you running from something?" Ordinarily, Osbourne would have found the notion laughable. Primeans fought, or they died. There was no in-between.

"Sickness, darkness. It takes the bears, too. I have seen them. More are coming. The ones in purple."

"What do you mean?" Osbourne knew that he had asked the question in vain; the gorilla's breathing became shallower with every second.

"Sickness, darkness. More land, more dis—" The Primean fell still.

Osbourne's mind raced to make sense of the cryptic words. Perhaps it was the naga who lived in the swamps on the border of Ursidaen and

Aldmist? If not them, who? Other Primeans? Other beasts entirely? Osbourne didn't know, couldn't come to a solid answer.

Still, the now-dead gorilla had all but admitted that the Primeans were invading Ursidaen... The realization struck Osbourne. This camp had only been a diversion so that a more significant force could pass by.

Osbourne turned around and started running back to his camp, hoping, praying, that Astrid was safe.

6

A chunk of lead formed in Osbourne's gut when he arrived back at the Ursidaen campsite as the bitter, earthy scents of more Primeans entered his nostrils. A moment later, his ears perked up at the sound of clashing steel, ringing and clangorous, off in the distance.

"Astrid..." Osbourne whispered. The polar bear picked up his pace, whispering a skaldic poem to grant himself a burst of vigor.

And then it came into view. Dawn had nearly vanquished the grip of twilight, illuminating the Ursidaen camp beyond. Gorillas surrounded it, and the bears fought to repulse the invaders.

"No," Osbourne growled, taking Olaf's axe in both paws. "It can't be..."

But it was. Osbourne sent himself hurtling toward the battle. A roar boomed from his mouth as he fell upon the nearest gorilla, bisecting the unfortunate beast with a brutal chop. Gore jetted from both halves as they dropped to the ground. Red ringed Osbourne's vision.

"Osbourne returns!" a grizzly bear cried out as she dueled with a gorilla.

Osbourne's gaze flitted about the tableau of pandemonium. Astrid was near the back, barely visible behind two Primeans who rained strike after strike upon her. Osbourne was already in motion, a poem on his lips:

"Tordok's lightning, pure and true,
wrath wielded by a chosen few,
fill your bears with godly might
that we drive our foes from sight!"

One gorilla dared to bar Osbourne's path; she lost her head with not even a moment's thought, the red stump of her neck ushering her vital fluids into the dirt. Another gorilla fell, and another. The rage clawed at Osbourne's mind in a bid to possess him; he held it back; he was so close to Astrid.

Osbourne's axe came down again, opening the spine of one of the gorillas attacking Astrid with a sickening crack. The other gorilla attacking Astrid turned around just in time for her to drive her sword through his neck.

"Ozzy," Astrid said, her voice ragged and relieved. "Thank the gods."

"We can do that once we are done with all of this." Osbourne turned around.

The gorillas mainly were pushed to the left edge of the camp now, forced further and further back by the rallied Ursidaens. Bror was at the front, his arms a blur of motion as he unleashed wrathful axe strikes and torrents of seething flame. The stench of charred flesh overtook all others. Behind the bears lay the bodies of their fallen fellows, six in total.

Osbourne clacked his teeth at the sight of the Ursidaen dead. They should have been alive and fighting. Osbourne pointed his axe at the gorillas and fed his anger to his Gift. His muscles writhed as electricity flowed through him, culminating in a lightning bolt that screamed forth and chained between the gorillas, smiting three of them dead. The rest were slain soon after.

As the smoke cleared and the battle ended, Osbourne's vision spun from dizziness. He felt as though he had been partially yanked from his body, and his throat was as dry as a desert. He forced himself back into focus with a deep breath. The rest of the warband was already walking toward him, Bror in the lead.

"See, Osbourne?" The grizzly bear wore a smug expression. "The *apes* are dead because we wield the very power they fear."

Osbourne nodded; every Ursidaen warrior knew that Primeans refused to use magic. Still, Osbourne wanted to claw the smile off Bror's face; the rage still whispered to the polar bear.

"What happened during your hunt?" Bror asked, taking a tone of diplomatic neutrality.

Osbourne held back a growl, but he didn't, couldn't, stop himself from glaring. It was obvious. He held up the berserker axe. Olaf's axe. "The same as what happened here, apparently. Beasts fought. Beasts died."

Whispers passed between the other bears. Astrid's expression became one of shock and concern at the sight of her mate painted in lacerations, his fur matted with gore, dirt, and worse, carrying a weapon of Ursidaen make that wasn't his own.

That Bror still managed to stand tall was a testament to his arrogance. "And here we stand victorious. Is there anything else you wish to tell us?"

Every word grated against Osbourne. Olaf was dead. Astrid could have been killed. The rage cried out for justice, and the Gift agreed. Osbourne gazed past Bror toward his mate and forced himself to take a deep breath. Astrid managed a melancholic, encouraging smile, and her eyes glimmered with freshly formed tears. Osbourne wished that he could throw himself into her embrace. He couldn't. He exhaled. For *her*, the rage and the Gift ceased their demands.

"The Primean camp Olaf and I found was a diversion," Osbourne said, "For this. I also learned that the gorillas are running from invaders in their own land, ones that are coming for us, too. I think they mean the naga."

Bror held Osbourne's gaze. "We have fought *apes* and *snakes* before. We held them back."

"Six more bears are dead today." Osbourne's tone was sharp and accusing.

"So are nearly a dozen *apes*, not counting your kills," Bror replied, "and now there will be ample trails to follow. We'll take today to recover and bury the dead, and then we will start moving again tomorrow at first light. We'll solve this predicament soon enough."

"No. This is clearly the start of something much larger than we can handle. We need to return to the pack and tell Kolvar what happened."

"Last I remember, Osbourne, I did not ask a question." Bror's tone became one of frigid authority.

"Nor did I, Trynjul Bror." Osbourne flexed his grip on Olaf's axe.

"Are you challenging my authority?" Bror heightened his posture.

"I have no choice but to." Osbourne's gaze flitted to Astrid and then back to Bror. "Seven warriors have died on your watch due to a poorly planned attack and an enemy ambush designed to take advantage of that, and now we have learned of another foe. Yet, you would have us press forward."

"In greater numbers, with all of us together," Bror countered, "Besides, after not one but two victories, the *apes'* hearts will surely be ripe with despair. We must capitalize now."

"Like they will be expecting us to do so that they can ambush us with a chariot, leave no survivors, and continue their invasion with Tordok knows what chasing them."

Bror gave a rich, deprecating laugh. "Again, a berserker shies away from battle. Looking as you are, I would have expected you to be hungering for more. *Apes* and *snakes* are easy work, after all."

Osbourne did indeed hunger for another battle, just not against the gorillas or whatever it was they were running from. "I speak for the good of the warband."

Bror looked at all of the other Ursidaens for a moment before continuing to speak, "All have heard that Usyling Osbourne speaks for the good of the warband, as is the obligation of every member, and so I will allow the warband to speak for itself." Bror paused as he looked once more at the gathered bears, allowing tension to build within the pregnant silence. "Who agrees with Osbourne?"

At first, none of the other Ursidaens moved. The tension in the air intensified. Osbourne looked to Astrid with a silent plea in his eyes.

She stepped forward and raised her paw. "I stand with Usyling Osbourne." Her voice split the air, and all eyes fell upon her, especially those of Bror.

He turned around to face Astrid fully. "Of course, you stand with your mate."

Hyddi, the other warrior-mage, stepped forward. "Through the divination granted to me by Akksardi," the black bear said, "I have learned that we will face only woe should we choose to pursue the Primeans now. Therefore, I stand with Usyling Osbourne as well, for the good of the warband."

Bror met Hyddi's gaze for a moment. It became a glare that swiveled about the warband. "No. We can still stop our foes." He paused. "All of them."

"Not when we do not know where they are, how many there are, or even what they are," Osbourne replied, slightly calmer now that Hyddi's divinations had confirmed what he already knew. "I know that you are eager to prove your worth. Kolvar has told me of your desire to command a Hafna. Still, that is no excuse for this recklessness. Olaf died because of it." Osbourne gestured with the axe that had once belonged to his fellow warrior.

Bror turned back around to face Osbourne with precision and poise that had been drilled into him by military training. "I have already tolerated your insubordination once, Osbourne. I will not do so again."

"I speak for the good of the warband."

"So you have said, but do you honestly think that denigrating my ambition is good for the warband?" Bror laughed sardonically. "Spare me, please. We are strong enough. Look at you, for example. You slew more *apes* by yourself than we did together, even before coming to our aid."

"And now, I am tired, and I am wounded. Another battle will put me on death's door." Osbourne paused. "It is folly for us to go on the offensive. We must return to Kolvar. However, you cannot accuse me of insubordination yet." Osbourne gestured to the rest of the warband. "Let every other bear speak their piece."

As if on cue, all of the other Ursidaens stepped forward and raised their paws in solidarity with Osbourne.

Bror appeared as though he had been struck by a hammer. The next moment passed in silence as his expression hardened into a scowl.

"Is that it then?" he asked, addressing the warband as a whole. "All of you now refuse to fight?"

"With all due respect, Trynjul Bror," Hyddi said, "The odds are against us. That is clear to see."

Bror shook his head. "No. The odds are not against us. I am simply surrounded by cowards, Ursidaens who call themselves Odolig, warriors, but do not know the true meaning of the title." The grizzly bear glared at each other Ursidaen in turn. "That will change, however. We will pursue the Primeans at first light tomorrow and make them regret ever setting foot in Ursidaen." Bror pulled his axe from his belt and raised it to the sky. Its steel head shone in the morning light. Then, it fell, pointing at Astrid. "And *she* will be at the front with us since Osbourne has been working so hard to make her battle-ready."

"No!" Osbourne snapped as he dropped Olaf's axe, pulled his own from his belt, and pointed it at Bror. "You cannot call us cowards and then demand that we follow you into assured destruction. For the good of this warband, Clan Eldingblod, and the nation of Ursidaen, I, Usyling Osbourne Gudbrandr, declare you, Trynjul Bror Halvarson, unfit for leadership and relieve you of your command."

Bror looked at Osbourne with a savage grin that bordered on bloodthirsty. "And now, that which I have known all along has become unquestioningly apparent. You are seeking to supplant me."

"You may call it whatever you wish. My challenge still stands."

"So it does, and I accept." Bror's grin widened. "Let us test your mettle and see if you are truly worthy of being Usyling."

"Only those who are not berserkers would dare to challenge one so brazenly." Osbourne unshouldered his shield, dropped his pack, and assumed a fighting stance that kept his axe close to his torso. "I think that it is your mettle that needs to be tested, Bror."

Bror's only response was a snarl of defiance as he, too, readied himself to fight.

7

A tense silence fell over the warband, and the gathered Ursidaens gave Osbourne and Bror a wide berth as they faced off. Under any other circumstances, it would have been an honor to watch them duel. Both the berserker and the warrior-mage were among the elite of the Ursidaen military.

Osbourne knew that the contest before him was far more than a duel between two warriors, and it was greater still than a mere conflict of authority.

It was a matter of life and death.

Osbourne saw it in the eyes of each of the other bears, especially Astrid. Her eyes were azure orbs of desperate hope and unconditional love. For *her*, Osbourne would fight no matter the odds, no matter how wounded he was, just as his father had.

Bror conjured a crackling orb of red-orange flames and hurled it at Osbourne. The berserker reflexively blocked with his shield; Bror's globe slammed into it and dissipated, leaving the shield blackened and smoking where the symbol of Tordok had been.

Osbourne lurched into a charge, hurtling toward Bror with a trio of ground-eating strides. The last of them saw Osbourne swinging his axe in an upward cleaving blow, red forming around his vision. Bror sidestepped, but Osbourne followed up with a shield bash that sent the grizzly bear staggering back. He quickly recovered and hacked at Osbourne with his axe. The polar bear blocked with his own, and the sound of ringing steel reverberated through the air as the weapons clashed. The next moments passed in a series of fierce exchanges, weapons grinding and snarling against each other before the combatants finally stepped back into defensive stances and began circling each other. The only reason Osbourne had not fallen into the rage was his own willpower.

"Put your pride aside, Bror," Osbourne said, "We can end this right now and return to the rest of our pack without shame."

Bror responded with his axe, beginning the melee anew by lunging and hacking at Osbourne. The berserker threw his shield in the way, blocking the blow as he retaliated with his own axe. Though Bror tried to dodge, Osbourne was already too close; his axe tore into Bror's armor, breaking through it but not drawing any blood.

The roar of flames was all that Osbourne heard next as Bror's free paw became ensorcelled in them, cannoning toward Osbourne's face. The polar bear rolled with the blow so that it only struck his shoulder. Pain blossomed in his flesh as his armor started to buckle under the heat. The red haze thickened. Osbourne stood his ground.

The trials to become a berserker had taught the polar bear a simple truth. If he could feel pain, he was alive. If he was alive, he could fight.

Osbourne threw his bulk into Bror, forcing the grizzly bear to yield more ground. Wasting no time in following up, Osbourne swung his axe. Bror met Osbourne's axe with his own, sending Osbourne's weapon flying from his grasp. It landed headfirst in a patch of dirt beyond the gathered Ursidaens.

Bror stepped back and pointed his axe at Osbourne. "I will accept your surrender now."

"I do not recall giving one," the polar bear rumbled back before lunging and cannoning his shield toward Bror.

The grizzly bear immediately threw a globe of fire at Osbourne. It slammed into his chest and threw him to the ground with its explosion, leaving a haze of smoke around him. Pressing his advantage, Bror slammed his hind paw on Osbourne's chest and pressed the edge of his axe against the polar bear's throat.

"Yield," Bror growled, "Now."

Osbourne did not; he would not let Astrid march on the frontlines of Bror's ill-fated crusade. Osbourne's vision turned resplendently sanguine as he gave himself over to the berserker rage. Letting out a roar, he latched onto Bror's paw with his own and tore it away, sending the grizzly bear's axe flying, neither seeing nor caring where it landed. Bror scrambled to react; Osbourne threw his foe off him as he rose to his hind paws. Another violent impulse saw lightning flash across the paw that had once held Osbourne's axe. Had he not been in the thrall of his rage, he would have asked for a surrender. Instead, Osbourne threw himself forward, leading with a shield bash that slammed into Bror's chest before following up with his lightning-wreathed paw.

Ensorcelling one of his own paws with fire, Bror caught Osbourne's. Fire and lightning clashed in a storm of wrath that mirrored that of their wielders, bathing the area in a light brighter than day. Both Osbourne and Bror roared as pain wracked their bodies and more smoke enshrouded them. Neither bear relented.

Bror recoiled his arm for another punch, but Osbourne moved faster, snatching his foe's throat in his grasp. Another moment saw Osbourne clamping down, shredding fur, skin, and flesh alike with his claws as blood gushed from between his fingers. Bror's expression was fixed in terror as his body was rendered lifeless. Osbourne gave one last squeeze to ensure that he had finished his work; the gore that soaked his paw and the red steam that billowed forth was not proof enough. He then threw Bror's corpse to the ground and let out a roar of victory.

No applause followed. The other bears bore looks of trepidation if not outright fear. All of them had heard tales of the brutality of which the berserkers were capable of, but few had witnessed it personally.

"Come back," Astrid said softly, beckoningly, as she strode toward her mate, her arms extended.

Osbourne's glare, filled with primal hatred and bloodlust, fell entirely upon Astrid.

She stood her ground. "Come back, Ozzy. Please."

Every fiber of Osbourne's body screamed for him to lash out and slay the latest foe, and the lightning about his paw snarled and crackled. He stepped toward Astrid.

Astrid stepped closer to Osbourne. "Bror is dead, Ozzy. Please, don't spill any more blood. I love you."

Through the crimson shroud that had fallen upon Osbourne's mind, Astrid's words came through as lucid whispers from beyond.

Blood... That was the word to which Osbourne clung the most. Grinning, he raised his paw to strike.

"Ozzy," Astrid pleaded. She had not shifted her stance in the slightest.

Her word, his name, cut through the crimson mist about the polar bear's mind like a blade of fire, consuming it utterly.

"Astrid," Osbourne whispered, sounding as though he had woken from a dream. He lowered his paw, and the lightning unraveled into disparate tendrils that skittered off into nonexistence.

"Ozzy." Astrid smiled, tears flowing down her face.

Osbourne embraced his mate. "Astrid." Her name was all he could say. He held her close for a long moment, finally releasing her with a kiss on her forehead.

Osbourne faced the rest of the warband. "I am back, and Bror is dead..." His voice trailed off into heavy silence as his gaze fell upon Bror's still-bleeding corpse. He again remembered his father.

"Had you not slain him," Váli said, "he would have slain you, and then he would have led us all into certain death."

Osbourne gave a heavy sigh. He did not want to admit the truth of his fellow berserker's words, but he could not deny it, either. What would Kolvar have to say about all of this? The next moments passed in silence.

"With Bror dead, who will lead us?" one of the other bears asked.

"I think Osbourne should," Váli replied.

Osbourne shook his head, his heart heavy with guilt. "No, not I."

"Yes, you, Osbourne." There was new vigor in Váli's voice, and the black bear stood taller. "It was you who demanded justice for every bear who died today because of Bror's poor leadership, and you staked your life on the matter. Bror knew that he could die when he fought you. He just did not think that he would. That was his mistake, and it is not your burden to bear. I choose you."

One by one, every other Ursidaen repeated the exact phrase in turn: "I choose you."

Osbourne sighed, forcing a slight smile despite his sadness and shame. "Very well then. I suppose I have no choice." He collected his axe, cleaned the weapon on the grass, and then he retrieved Olaf's weapon.

"Aye, now you got it," Váli replied, "What is your first order?"

Osbourne suppressed a yawn as he fastened his axe on his belt. Fatigue was quickly coming over him now that the threat had passed. "Build a fire. We must give everyone a proper burial."

It took only a few minutes for the Ursidaens to build a funeral pyre, a blazing pillar at the center of the camp in which all of the bodies were placed, both Ursidaen and Primean, one after another, still bearing armor and weapons. No eulogy was given. All of the bears simply watched until Bror's body, the last to be burned, could no longer be seen, at which point the fire was doused with dirt.

"It is done," Osbourne said, "Bror's spirit is with the gods."

"And now we can return to Kolvar," Astrid said.

Osbourne looked around at the wounded, ragged, weary bears, then back at Astrid. "No." Turning to the warband, Osbourne said, "I think we should spend the rest of the day here, recuperate, and start again tomorrow at first light. However, I want double watches during the night. What do you think, Hyddi? Does your Gift say that we should do otherwise?"

"The future is in great flux..." The black bear's voice trailed off. "Weal and woe are equally likely, but I think your plan is sound, Osbourne. We should attend to our wounded before we try to travel."

"Very well," Osbourne replied, "Thank you, Hyddi."

Murmurs of agreement from the other bears followed, and the least wounded took the first watch. The rest returned to their tents, including Osbourne and Astrid.

Osbourne sighed as he sat down and looked into Astrid's eyes. There was a hard knot in his chest. "I am sorry... about what happened out there. I—"

Astrid gently laid a paw over Osbourne's mouth. "You've nothing to apologize for, love. I stood with you the first time you fell into the rage, and I stand with you now. I will never leave you."

Osbourne was dumbstruck; he couldn't divorce himself from the guilt. He knew that he had had to kill Bror to keep Astrid safe, but he should have had better control. He had come precariously close to striking his mate. Had he done so, she would have ended up worse than Olaf, dead by his paw.

Astrid nuzzled Osbourne's face and kissed him on the cheek. "You are the best mate I could have asked for, and nothing you say or do will change that."

It was as though the words had opened a floodgate. "Thank you," Osbourne whispered, his voice trembling. He pulled Astrid into a tight embrace as tears trailed down his muzzle.

Astrid let Osbourne weep as long as he needed to. They did not leave their tent for the rest of the day.

And then, they slept.

8

"Osbourne, Astrid, wake up!" roared a bear. "We're under attack!"

Osbourne and Astrid jolted upright. Immediately, they began preparing for battle, donning their armor and taking up their weapons as fast as their limbs would let them. The clash of steel against steel echoed beyond.

Emerging from their tent, Osbourne and Astrid were confronted by the sight of Ursidaens battling... other Ursidaens? Osbourne perished his questions. Hyddi was already on the ground, twitching.

Osbourne immediately rushed over to her, and Astrid was not far behind.

"Hyddi," Osbourne said as he knelt before the Trynjul.

Her armor had been cut open to reveal a jagged gash across her chest that was bleeding liberally.

"Osbourne..." Hyddi could manage only a hoarse whisper.

"Mother Fjardi," Osbourne began, "come to me now..."

Hyddi raised her paw. "It is too late for me, but the battle continues. You must protect the others, Os—"

Hyddi gave her last breath and fell limp. Osbourne knew that she would not rise again. The polar bear rose, Olaf's axe in his paws, and a song imbued with skaldic power boomed from his mouth as he strode forward:

"Eternal light never dies!

Join me, brethren, in this cry!

No challenge do we fear,

for the price of our lives is dear

By fang and claw and axe,

Justice is served!

Join me, brethren,

in driving the foe back!

With Tordok's might in our paws

and his lightning in our hearts,

we deliver ourselves to victory!

Eternal light never dies!"

The air thickened like a brewing storm with every word Osbourne sang. A new wellspring of vigor flowed through him, and his Gift answered the display of skaldic might, his axe becoming a beacon of radiance as its head was cocooned in howling lightning. All around, the other bears of Osbourne's warband were fighting harder and faster from the new ferocity blooming within them, adding their own roars to the last line of the song:

"Eternal light never dies!"

Osbourne's axe careened toward his foe, another polar bear, but unlike any Osbourne had seen before. Her eyes gleamed with insanity and hatred entwined, and patches of her fur were missing, instead playing host to clusters of gnarled, black growths, some with tiny teeth sprouting from them. Instinctually, Osbourne recognized the corruption of dark magic, and his disgust amplified his wrath.

The corrupted bear parried with her own axe, the weapon keening as Osbourne's lightning sheered through it, sending the head falling to the ground. Continuing on its course, Osbourne's axe plowed into his foe's chest, steel whining as her breastplate was slashed and crumpled, the force of the blow sending her staggering back. Red ringed Osbourne's vision as he lunged and made the mortal strike, a cleaving blow that sent his foe's head flying amid a fountain of blood. The headless body unceremoniously collapsed. A kernel of guilt formed within Osbourne as he found himself grinning at the dead beast.

It felt good to wield a berserker's axe again.

All around, the storm of fangs, claws, and steel raged, and Osbourne was its eye. Astrid was to Osbourne's left, furiously trading blows with another corrupted bear. Osbourne strode toward his mate, and a roar erupted from his throat as he carved into the side of his latest foe, releasing a gory deluge. Astrid finished the corrupted bear with a thrust that sent her blade through his throat.

"Come on, Ozzy," Astrid said as she pulled her sword free. "I was handling him just fine."

Osbourne glanced down at the corpse. The dead bear's face was a mask of savage glee. Osbourne's gaze returned to Astrid. "This is not a training exercise."

Together, the two polar bears ensconced themselves in another section of the battle, aiding their fellows in cutting down more of their foes, triumphant roars following every kill. The rage pulsed and ticked inside Osbourne's head, begging to be free, and still he held it back. His mate was right next to him, and—

A shield crashing into Osbourne's back sent pain surging through him like a tidal wave; he cried out as he whirled around to face his latest foe. The corrupted bear's axe was already whistling toward him. He jolted back, feeling the whoosh of air against his throat as he narrowly evaded the strike. Another corrupted bear joined the first, wearing a rot-ripe grin as she swung a giant, flanged maul right at Osbourne's face, forcing him back further.

He swung his axe, and a lightning bolt screamed forth, slamming into the bear with the axe and shield. The maul wielder swung again. Osbourne sidestepped and cannoned his hind paw into the bear's chest, sending her staggering back as her armor groaned from the impact. A third bear joined the fray, and Osbourne could deny the berserker rage no longer. He let out a pandemonic roar as his whole world turned red.

* * *

Osbourne's head was too light. His body was too heavy. It was as though he were looking at the world through a shimmering veil. The battle was over. Corpses twisted by dark magic were strewn about all over the camp, and Osbourne's eyes widened as he realized that there were both bears and gorillas. Amid the carnage, the bears of Osbourne's warband tended the wounded and mourned the dead.

And Astrid was nowhere to be found. Osbourne's heartbeat picked up as a new, harsh lucidity crashed down upon him. He saw everything in perfect detail, and... Astrid was still gone.

"Where is she?" Osbourne whispered. They had been together only a few minutes ago, fighting the corrupted bears. But, that had been before the rage. Osbourne could only guess how much time had passed since then.

He walked over to Váli, who was cleaning his axe. The black bear stopped and rose to his full height.

"They aren't naga, but these," Váli gestured to the corpses all around, "these were what you were told about, aren't they? These are what the Primeans are running from."

"Yes," Osbourne admitted, wishing that he had been correct. For as much as he disliked the naga, he had fought them before. He knew them. These other bears... They had once been proud warriors of Ursidaen, reduced to Tordok knew what. And gorillas, too? Osbourne shook his head and forced himself to breathe, returning his focus to the most urgent matter. "Have you seen Astrid?"

"She's not with any of the others?" Váli replied.

"Not that I could see." A chunk of lead formed in Osbourne's gut. If Váli didn't know, none of the others would, either.

Váli sighed. "I wish I could help you, Osbourne. I really do."

"Thank you." Osbourne's voice was hollow.

He stalked through the camp, checking every patch of ground, and found a trail of three sets of paws leading out of the camp to the east. Osbourne's stomach twisted as he recognized the familiar scent wafting up from the central set of tracks. Even without the scent, he would have recognized Astrid's pawprints anywhere.

Osbourne returned to Váli. "I must go." His voice was heavy with desperation.

"Do you want any of us to come with you?" Váli asked.

"No." Osbourne shook his head. "I need to move as quickly as possible. You are the leader of the warband now, Váli. Return to Kolvar, and—" Osbourne handed over Olaf's axe. "—make sure this gets back to Tyra."

Váli nodded. "I will, Osbourne. May Tordok light your way."

"Thank you."

Part II: Heart of Darkness

9

"Astrid!" Osbourne's gaze darted about, finding no sign of his partner through the blinding snowstorm.

Osbourne trudged forward. His heart pounded, and his blood raced. He sped up at the sight of a vaguely bear-like silhouette ahead. "Astrid, I am coming!"

"Osbourne!" Astrid's voice soared above the keening wind, and the silhouette quivered. "Osbourne, help me!"

Osbourne's throat went dry as the silhouette faded into the austere whiteness all around. "Astrid! Astrid, where are you?"

All that came back was more keening wind, a wordless mockery.

*   *   *

Osbourne awoke. Cold sweat matted his fur, and his bones and muscles throbbed with aches. Wearily, he blinked. A fog hung over his mind. It was hard to believe that he was still in the snow cave that he had dug the previous evening. Astrid had been so close.

Three days had passed since Osbourne had left his warband behind, and yet the memories of his fellow bears already seemed distant. It had seemed so simple at the start: find the encroaching Primeans and learn what their purpose was. Now...

Osbourne's bones cracked and popped as he rose upright into a sitting position. He quenched his thirst with a mouthful of snow, mulching it slowly. The sensation of water running down his throat was not as refreshing as he wanted it to be. He reached next for a chunk of raw meat buried in the snow and began to eat. The meat was stiff, stringy, and tasteless save for what little flavor was offered by the gobbets of frozen blood upon it. Osbourne finished the scant meal in a few large bites, unconcerned with the fact that it was all that remained of his last hunt. He would find more.

The polar bear put on his armor, took up his axe and shield, and egressed from his snow cave. The landscape was pure white, broken only by small patches of tall grass and the occasional leafless tree. Osbourne had no trail to follow, either, having lost it after the first snow, but he refused to turn back. If nothing else, he took the dream as an omen that he was still headed in the right direction.

Seconds became minutes. Minutes became hours. All Osbourne could see was more snow and more grass, and all he could smell was the cold, crisp air. Despair welled up within the polar bear and the notion that his search for Astrid had failed gnawed at him.

No. He would not give up on his mate. She would not give up on him if the positions were reversed. He shook his head. No, Astrid would not give up on him. He pressed on.

From off in the distance emerged vaguely bestial forms, standing upright. Osbourne could not tell what kind of beasts they were, but they were moving slowly in his general direction. Perhaps they were other Ursidaens? Osbourne hoped to Akksardi that they were. He picked up his pace.

Closer and closer, the polar bear came, his hope rising with every stride. Then, he stopped, his hope giving way to dismay. There were gorillas and bears together. The group continued to move toward Osbourne, but he could not tell whether or not they had spotted him. Without consciously thinking about it, he pulled his axe from his belt.

He watched for a few more moments. The other beasts came closer, and Osbourne wrinkled his nose as the deathly stench of dark magic wafted into his nostrils. And still, they had not noticed him; the corruption seemed to have rotted their minds as well as their bodies.

Osbourne knew that his good fortune would not, could not, last much longer. And there was nowhere to hide. Osbourne started walking to the right, carving a wide semicircle around the bears and gorillas. As he nearly passed by them, one of the corrupted stopped and looked over its shoulders, its gaze falling upon Osbourne. A wordless snarl followed as the corrupted beast pointed its weapon at the polar bear. As one, the others turned around and charged.

Osbourne's heart pounded as he counted his foes. Nine. There would be no winning if he fought them head-on, even with the might of his Gift and his rage, not with how he had not fully recovered from his previous battles. Turning around, the polar bear broke into a run, throwing up snow behind him as the corrupted beasts ran in pursuit.

Soon, they were tiny, perhaps the size of Osbourne's paw, and a cluster of vaguely triangular shapes jutting up from the snow came into view ahead. Another camp? Osbourne kept running, not looking back. A burning sensation writhed within the polar bear's legs, and his armor and weapons became heavier and heavier.

"Through Tordok's might, I persevere," Osbourne growled, calling upon his skaldic power. "Through Tordok's vigor, I will prevail!" The burning and the heaviness lessened as Osbourne began moving faster.

The shapes ahead became clearer. They were tents of Ursidaen make, lopsided and torn. Osbourne's new vigor fled as he entered the camp, crushed by despair at the desolation before him. There were no other beasts, though trails of pawprints ran every which way, and there were patches of blackened earth ringed by rocks. Osbourne looked around for any signs of heraldry that might indicate what clan the camp had belonged to. He found none.

His ears perked up at one of the tents starting to rustle. He turned around and was confronted by a corrupted bear darting out. Its hateful eyes stared straight through Osbourne, and many clumps of its brown fur had fallen out, revealing flesh ravaged by rot.

Anger reared up inside Osbourne. Lightning fulminated into existence about the head of his axe as he called upon his Gift and assumed a fighting stance. The clash lasted for only a few moments before Osbourne felled his foe with a strike of his axe, screeching lightning shredding the air.

The fetid stench rising from the corpse twisted Osbourne's stomach. Despite his disgust, he found himself staring into the lifeless eyes of his former foe. The bear had once been a fellow warrior and had not deserved such a horrific fate. How had such a thing even happened? Osbourne also could not help but wonder if he had met the other bear at some point in the past. He reached for the fallen warrior's shield.

There were many cracks, nicks, and gouges upon it, and the paint was faded, but a symbol was still visible. It was the roaring head of a polar bear flanked by crossed yellow lightning bolts. A chunk of lead formed in Osbourne's gut. That was one of the symbols of Clan Eldingblod. His clan.

A bevy of questions formed in Osbourne's mind. Which town had this bear come from? Where were the other bears in the warband? Were they still sane, or had they suffered the same wretched fate? Had Astrid come across this same camp, too? Osbourne gulped at the potential answers to the last question but pushed them down. Dwelling on them brought him no closer to knowing what had happened.

With a sigh, Osbourne pulled his gaze away from the body and began walking toward one of the other tents in the camp. Inside, he found unrolled blankets and a bulging backpack. Guilt hardened in his chest as he reached for the backpack. It was wrong to take from the fallen, but he needed the supplies. Grasping the strap, Osbourne pulled the backpack closer and opened it, taking an inventory of the contents. There was bread, hard cheese, dried meat and fruit, two waterskins, flint and steel, and bandages.

"Forgive me, Akksardi." Osbourne rolled up the blankets and tied them to the pack, at which point he closed the pack, slung it over his shoulder, and left the tent.

He checked the other tents next. All of them were in a similar state of disarray, and none of them were occupied. The absences invoked grief in Osbourne.

The polar bear returned to the fallen warrior, and he dragged the corpse to the nearest fire ring, grunting and huffing from the exertion. He then took out the flint and steel from his pack, knowing that lighting a fire would signal the other corrupted beasts. Osbourne did not care. His fellow Odolig deserved a proper funeral. He lit the corpse with a few harsh strikes of flint and steel. The flames took hold quickly, blanketing the fallen warrior in crackling orange, yellow, and white. Staring solemnly into the pyre, Osbourne gave a eulogy:

"Though I did not know your name,
you are of my clan, Clan Eldingblod,
 and a proud warrior of Ursidaen.
To Tordok's realm you go."

The flames consumed the body and the leather armor upon it over the next minutes, leaving behind only the charred husks of what had once been the warrior's axe and shield. Osbourne then doused the flames with snow, hissing steam bursting up. Once the steam had dissipated, Osbourne went back to the edge of the camp from which he had come. There were no foes in sight. Turning back around, he passed through the camp one last time before leaving it behind, trying not to become overwhelmed by gnawing desperation.

Astrid had to be out there. She had been taken alive for a reason, right? Osbourne had to believe that. If it wasn't true… The polar bear gulped. He had already failed once.

He would not fail again.

10

Osbourne pressed on until well after daylight had retreated beneath the southern horizon. His legs burned with every step, and his whole body ached from the load he was carrying, but the notion of stopping did not enter his mind. Exhaustion be damned, he had to keep moving.

The polar bear covered a few hundred more feet before the pain became too much, making each step seem like an act of the gods. Still, he did not want to allow himself the luxury of rest, not when he was still on the open snow where the corrupted beasts could find him. He gritted his teeth as he forced himself ever forward. He had to find a place where he could dig a cave.

Smoke wafted into his nostrils, reinvigorating him. Was there another bear living in this desolation? As Osbourne continued forward, a flickering orange light appeared amid the darkness.

"Kraan's light guides me forward," Osbourne whispered, "Kraan's light shows me the way."

The light became larger and larger, coming from a fire within a hut of earth and wood with a thatch roof, two windows, and a circular door. Osbourne could hardly believe his eyes. Another beast really did live out here in the middle of nowhere.

He stopped in front of the door and knocked. "Hello?"

"Who goes there?" The responding voice was that of a female bear, worn and rickety from age.

"I am Osbourne Gudbrandr of Clan Eldingblod, and I humbly ask for shelter. I have traveled quite far."

"Enter and be welcome. I will not refuse a fellow Ursidaen."

Osbourne smiled wearily. Finally, something had gone right. He gently pushed open the door. It creaked as it yielded to him, revealing a bright hearth and the shadowed forms of a table, chairs, a bed, and an occupied rocking chair. Slowly, the polar bear passed through the threshold, closing the door behind him.

"Please, have a seat." The bear in the rocking chair gestured to her table and the chair that was pushed into it.

"Thank you," Osbourne said as he seated himself and unshouldered his shield and backpack.

"It is I who should be thanking you. It is rare that I get company these days."

Now that he was closer to the fire, Osbourne could see his benefactor more clearly. She was a small black bear in a green homespun robe. Age had etched lines in her face and dulled her fur. Her paws were gnarled and bony. "If I may be so bold, why do you live out here?" Osbourne said, "I encountered Ursidaens and Primeans corrupted by dark magic not long ago."

The crone nodded sagely. "Aye. There have been more and more of them as of late." She paused, turning her gaze to the fire for a solemn moment. "They have not found me yet, thank Fjardi."

"Is there any hope for erasing the corruption and changing them back?" Osbourne cocked his head.

"I am afraid not." The elder bear shook her head. "I am an oracle of Fjardi." She held out her left paw, and it began to glow with golden light. "I have tried to break the enchantment. Every attempt ended in failure."

Osbourne's eyes widened as a wave of calm came over him, and his own Gift started to stir in the presence of such power. "I do not wish to impose, but since you are so blessed by the goddess of life, I am hoping that you can help me."

"Perhaps, but first, let me introduce myself and provide hospitality. My name is Bodil Vjarnen. Help yourself to the stew in the pot. Bowls and spoons are atop the mantel. You can use my bed when you are ready to sleep. I rarely leave this chair anymore. My bones do not take kindly to it when I do. Then, in the morning, we can discuss why you have come here and if I can help you."

"Thank you." The thought of not pressing on in his search for a whole night needled Osbourne, but he could not deny that he needed the food and rest that Bodil offered. That was why he had entered.

The polar bear rose from his chair and lumbered over to the hearth, mindful of every step so that he didn't knock over anything. Taking a bowl and spoon, he served himself from the stew pot. The smell was of tender beef basking in garlic, pepper, and rosemary, far better than the rations in his pack. Osbourne returned to his chair and took his first bite, immediately smiling. It was more delicious than he had expected. His stomach growled for more. Voraciously, he devoured his first bowl.

"May I," he began.

Bodil chuckled and gave a dismissive wave of her paw. "You may eat as much as you like, Osbourne. I can tell it has been too long since you have had a decent meal."

Osbourne ate two more bowls before he finally felt content. Afterward, he removed his axe and armor, setting them next to his pack, at which point he padded over to Bodil's bed, letting out a loud yawn as he laid down. He barely heard the older bear's chuckle.

Covering himself in the blankets, Osbourne soon drifted off. The last thing he saw was a tiny, golden panther face with twinkling, amethyst eyes staring at him from the mantel.

*   *   *

The light of a fresh spring dawn bathed the grasslands. Osbourne and Astrid were the only ones there, circling each other. Their armor clanked with every step; their shields were raised; their weapons were brandished.

"Come on, Ozzy," Astrid said mockingly, "No holding back this time."

"Do you think you can handle it?" Osbourne replied with a chuckle.

"How will I know if you never let me?"

"Alright then. Let us test your mettle!" Osbourne lunged and cleaved at Astrid with his axe.

She deftly blocked with her shield, wood cracking as it absorbed Osbourne's blow. Astrid flowed elegantly into a thrust of her sword, the weapon's razor-sharp point darting toward Osbourne's throat. Osbourne sidestepped and swung his axe low, aiming at Astrid's knee. She moved to parry but was a moment too slow, yelping as Osbourne's axe tore through her leather armor and bit into her flesh, and she fell to the ground as blood fountained from the wound.

*   *   *

Osbourne jolted awake, covered in cold sweat. He was still covered in Bodil's blankets, lying on Bodil's bed inside of Bodil's hut. The light of dawn peaked through the windows, and the fire inside the hearth had died down to mere embers. Bodil herself was rocking in her chair, her eyes closed.

Good. Osbourne took a deep breath, savoring the visceral sensation of his lungs expanding. It had only been a dream. And yet, he felt closer to Astrid. His gaze flitted down toward a stout iron handle on the floor near the bed. Not far from it was the distinct outline of a hatch, no doubt leading to Bodil's pantry. Exhaling, Osbourne sat up, rubbed his eyes, and yawned.

"How did you sleep?" Bodil asked.

"Fine," Osbourne lied, standing up from the bed and starting to stretch. His muscles ached, and his joints popped. Strangely, his wounds were now nearly scars, his previous scabs gone.

Bodil smiled.

The next minutes passed in silence as Osbourne continued his stretches, the same routine he did every morning before he and Astrid started sparring. The fact that he and Astrid weren't doing that put a void in his chest. He tried not to think about it.

Osbourne then had a cold breakfast from his rations. He offered to share with Bodil, but she declined.

"So, Osbourne," Bodil said once he had finished his meal, "what brings you all the way out here?"

"I am looking for my mate, Astrid," Osbourne replied, "She was taken by a pack of corrupted beasts. I initially went east to follow her, but now..." He sighed.

"I am truly sorry for your plight." Bodil smiled sympathetically. "You are not the first to have come to me with such a story. There may be a way I can help you, but I cannot guarantee that Astrid is still alive."

Osbourne ignored the twist in his stomach. "I understand. But first, I would like to know the other stories you have heard. Have any of the other beasts been successful? How long has this been happening?"

"It has been going on for many years, though I am ignorant of the source. As for the tales themselves, as I have said, they are similar to yours, and I do not know if any of those beasts reunited with their loved ones. I helped them as much as I could, just as I will do for you."

"I will accept whatever help you can give."

"Come here and take my paws." Bodil sat up straighter.

Osbourne obeyed. Bodil's paws were small and frail; Osbourne held them lightly. Bodil closed her eyes and began to whisper. Osbourne could not make out the words. He was not sure that Bodil was speaking Ursidaen. The oracle's paws soon glowed with a vibrant, yellow-green light, intensifying as she continued her incantation. After a few more moments, she finished, and the glow faded.

An image formed within Osbourne's mind. It was Astrid. She was caught in a snowstorm and desperately fighting off bears and gorillas. Shadows encroached all around.

Osbourne's heart beat faster. Astrid was still alive, and he knew now that she was somewhere to the north. Osbourne let go of Bodil's paws, walked over to where he had laid his possessions, and began putting on his armor.

"Thank you," he said to Bodil, "Thank you very much."

Bodil nodded. "There is but one last thing I wish to tell you."

"What is that?"

"Darkness will always find a way to spread itself."

Osbourne shuddered as he finished readying himself. "Thank you, Bodil Vjarnen. Your kindness will not be forgotten."

"It warms my heart to hear those words, Osbourne. Go with my blessing."

The polar bear wanted to say something more, but nothing came to him. What was a beast supposed to say when he was about to go forth to face death itself? Osbourne walked to the door, opened it, and lingered for another moment, his gaze locked with Bodil's. What seemed to be melancholy swirled in her eyes.

Finally, Osbourne left, closing the door behind him.

11

Fresh snow had fallen during the night, an undulating landscape of pure white sprawling out before Osbourne. He took his first step forward before he had consciously willed himself to. For the next hours, the polar bear's only companions were the clear sky overhead and the gentle wind.

Daylight dipped beneath the horizon and yielded to twilight easily, too easily, but Osbourne was still as vigorous and purposeful as he had been upon leaving Bodil's hut. He had not used any of his skaldic calls, either. Perhaps Bodil's enchantment was doing more than merely guiding him along his path

Osbourne stopped as he crested the next hill. Below stood many hulking, shadowy figures, barely visible under the bruised purple sky. It appeared as though they were gathered around something, but Osbourne could not make out what it was between the distance and the darkness. He could not even see how many figures there actually were. The one thing he was certain of was that they were corrupted beasts.

A sharp caw from on high shattered Osbourne's concentration; a griffon rife with bruise-colored sores and dark growths ridden by an equally infected bear flew toward the berserker. The air around Osbourne turned heavy as his Gift reared up, spurred by the adrenaline now rushing through him. He outstretched his paw, and his muscles tensed as electricity ran through them, manifesting as a lightning bolt. It slashed through the darkness, illuminating every deformity upon the polar bear's foes. A sickening crack sounded off a moment later as the lightning bolt smote the griffon, sending it and its rider falling to the ground. Osbourne's entwined anger and bewilderment fueled another lightning bolt that smote the rider, leaving a miasma of acrid smoke where its head had once been.

Snow crunched as the griffon hit the ground, and its motionless rider tumbled off. Osbourne pulled his axe from his belt and charged. The griffon rose as the polar bear closed the distance; Osbourne and his foe lunged at the same time. The griffon's beak perforated Osbourne's breastplate only to be stopped by the leathers beneath while Osbourne's axe sheered through the griffon's neck. Its head plopped unceremoniously into the snow, rot-rich gore spraying from the wound, soon followed by the rest of its body.

Osbourne took a deep breath, unshouldering his shield as he exhaled. He then turned toward his other foes. They were advancing. Osbourne gritted his teeth as he called upon his Gift for a third time. His vigor was ebbing, but he had no choice. The corrupted beasts would give nothing less than their all.

"By Tordok's axe!" Osbourne raised his axe, and the invisible force of the Gift coursed through him, so many strands coalescing into his weapon. A fresh crack split the air as bright blue lightning coruscated across the axe's head, all of its runes glowing balefully.

Osbourne snapped his arm forward, catapulting the lightning toward his foes and striking down the frontmost of the abominations. If the others noticed, they gave no sign of it. Fatigue coiled in Osbourne's muscles now; his axe, shield, and armor were becoming heavier, and his Gift retreated deeper inside him. He clacked his teeth together as he assumed a defensive stance. He could not, would not, allow himself to be stopped by these corrupted beasts. Triumph was his only option. He would cut them down, every last one of them, and then he would see them reduced to ashes in a funeral pyre.

"To Tordok's realm they go," Osbourne growled to himself.

His thoughts grew ever more violent, filled with visions of a battle that was but moments away. Crimson ringed his vision; Osbourne allowed it to rise. If ever there was a time to give in, it was now. The march of the corrupted beasts, jaunty and inexorable, set the rhythm to which Osbourne psyched himself up, becoming more and more of a madbeast amid his fit of snarling and growling and teeth clacking, his vision becoming redder and redder. The color of living blood and the passion that his foes lacked. The color of Osbourne's deliverance.

The corrupted beasts were now coming up the hill, wordlessly snarling and growling, their weapons swinging like pendulums. Osbourne found their stench stimulating; it was all he could do to not just throw himself at the abominations. Just a moment longer...

Now! The corrupted beasts were halfway up the hill when Osbourne charged, letting out a bloodcurdling roar that would have made any other foe reconsider their odds. The polar bear's axe collided first with another axe, then with the chest of one of his foes, caving it in, blood spraying. Whirling around, Osbourne bashed another corrupted beast with his shield, sending it crumpling to the ground. He did not know how many more there were. He did not care. He was home.

The corrupted beasts retaliated with their axes and swords, blades whistling as they careened toward Osbourne. He beat back two with his shield and one with his axe, splintering wood and ringing steel starting the next verse of the din of battle. Two more axes screeched as they scored Osbourne's breastplate, and leather snapped as a sword bit into the polar bear's shoulder. The warmth of flowing blood followed while the coppery tang of Osbourne's own vital fluids wafted into his nostrils. He did not feel any pain.

The berserker howled as he unleashed a wrathful cleave, opening the midsection of one foe, slicing into the chest of a second, and ripping through the rusted chainmail of a third. Another barrage of blades followed. Osbourne could only block two. The others hammered into his chest, shoulders, and one of his thighs, forcing him to yield step after step to the precious ground; he remained standing by sheer might. One of the corrupted beasts lunged to press the advantage, but Osbourne tore open its throat with his axe.

The rest of the corrupted beasts swung again. Osbourne charged into the strikes, ferociously repulsing them with titanic sweeps of his axe and shield, roars of defiance booming from his mouth. So ensconced was he in his rage that all their forms blurred together. One fell to the polar bear's axe, then another. The remaining foes flailed their axes and shields.

Osbourne blocked with his own shield, grinning savagely as blades became stuck in the wood of his shield. As the corrupted beasts pulled their weapons free, Osbourne's axe arm snapped forward, felling one of the abominations, then another. It was then that he realized there was only one foe left; it was swinging at him with its newly freed axe. Osbourne caught the weapon's blade with the rim of his shield and rolled with the blow, propelling himself into a sweep of his axe that sent the last corrupted beast's head flying from its shoulders. His foe slain, Osbourne roared in triumph and began searching for the next. He saw none. As the rage thickened from wrath denied, Osbourne remembered Astrid. Her cerulean eyes. Her dazzling smile. The way she called him "Ozzy." The redness in Osbourne's vision began to fade as lucidity returned to him. He took a deep breath.

"To Tordok's realm they go," he said as he exhaled. The rest of the red faded away.

Osbourne shouldered his shield and reaffixed his axe to his belt. He then dragged the corpses into a pile. It was grueling work, and his shoulder was throbbing and burning from his still-bleeding wound. Once his grim task was done, Osbourne reached inward toward his Gift. He did not need much for what he needed to do. Thin tendrils of lightning, a spiderweb of pure energy, skittered across Osbourne's paw. Focusing harder, he willed the lightning to flow toward the mound of carcasses before him. It obeyed. First, there were sparks, then flashes, and then fire, orange and vibrant, Tordok's mercy made manifest.

The flames reached ever higher, twisting, turning, swirling, dancing. Osbourne watched with satisfaction. His work was done. Knowing that the fire would eventually burn out on its own, the polar bear walked around it and down the hill.

12

Aches dogged Osbourne's every step. Another day of harsh marching and another night of dreams filled with haunting visions of Astrid had come and gone. Osbourne found a small measure of relief in the fact that he had not encountered any more corrupted beasts since the funeral pyre, though he almost wished that he had, just so that he could have the rush of battle to hold back the inexorable sense of despair.

He crested the next hill and stopped, his jaw dropping as he took in sight at the bottom. There were corpses strewn about. They were distinctly serpentine, having thick, coiling tails in place of legs. The males were muscular, nearly matching an Ursidaen in bulk, and scales covered their whole body, the colors ranging between shimmering hues of blue, green, and purple. A spiked fin, the same color as the scales but darker, ranged from the tops of their heads to the ends of their tails. Two smaller such fins extended from their forearms, and their webbed hands ended in tiny claws.

The females were shorter and lither, and their scales yielded at the shoulders, torso, and waist to smooth skin of a shade between marble and ivory. They had four arms rather than the two possessed by the males, and those limbs had neither scales nor fins nor claws. The females' back fins, starting at the tops of their heads, ended just before their rattle-crowned tails did.

All of the corpses had been painted with lacerations, and their sundered armor and broken weapons told a wordless story of a desperate struggle. A few of them were perforated with bite marks.

Osbourne immediately recognized the creatures as naga. Were they fleeing the same corruption afflicting the bears and gorillas? Osbourne's heart skipped a beat as he noticed that tiny horns and gangrenous growths had started to bloom on some of the naga. If that was the case... Aldmist was perhaps a day's journey away, two at most. Were the lizards suffering, too?

Hesitantly, Osbourne closed the distance to the naga. One of them, a blue-scaled male, was still twitching, clutching his spear close to his chest. Osbourne's eyes widened. Under ordinary circumstances, he might have left the naga to die or perhaps mercy-killed him, but the current conflict went beyond boundaries as arbitrary as clan or species and a living companion to travel with... Few things could match the value of that.

"Can you hear me?" Osbourne asked, speaking slowly and clearly. Some naga learned how to speak Ursidaen, just as some bears learned to understand the naga language, though they were physically incapable of speaking it.

The naga twitched faster, his back fin rising. His face turned slightly toward Osbourne, though his eyes were still closed.

There was no denying it now. The naga, though wounded, was definitely still alive.

"Can you hear me?" Osbourne reiterated, making sure that his paws were visible.

Slowly, the naga's eyes opened. He blinked a few times. As he opened his eyes again, he jolted back, pointing his spear at Osbourne. "Stay away, bear!"

"Let us have none of that," Osbourne said warningly, "I mean you no harm."

The naga glared at Osbourne before finally conceding, "Fine. Where are those... those abominations?"

"I took care of them." Osbourne extended his paw toward the naga. "Let me help you up."

The naga took Osbourne's paw, his hands colder than ice in the polar bear's grasp. Osbourne hefted the naga up in one strong, relatively smooth movement.

"Let us see about finding shelter now," Osbourne said, trying to keep his voice calm. Though he knew his suggestion was practical, he did not want to stop. Astrid was still out there, somewhere.

The naga nodded his agreement.

The wounded pair set a slow pace, ensuring that no foes crept up on them. They eventually found another hill and set up a meager camp behind it. Osbourne then built a small fire and shared his rations and blankets with the naga. The naga cocooned itself in the blankets close to the fire and ate slowly, his face twisting as he encountered tastes that he had never had before. Osbourne wolfed his portion down in a few pawfuls, letting out a sigh of relief afterward and fighting back a yawn.

"You are not like others of your kind," the naga said after he had finished eating.

"What makes you say that?" Osbourne asked.

"Any others would have left me for dead."

"Aye, the relations between our two species are not the best, but, this time our foe is the same. What were you doing so far from Lake Skalinnsjo?"

"Lake Skalinnsjo? I've never heard that name before." The naga paused. "Wait, that must be your kind's name for Zs'hhhesha." The naga gave a hissing laugh at Osbourne's perplexed expression; the polar bear was not even going to try to repeat that name. "Anyway," the naga continued, "I am one of the shamans of my tribe, and I was guiding a group of warriors on their vision quest. The divination I had performed before setting off foretold that the journey would be challenging, but nothing like what we encountered. There were so many of them..." The naga shook his head. "Haashan, who is like a son to me, was taken by the abominations but not killed immediately, for what purpose I do not know." The naga paused. "The vision quest was to determine his place within our clan. I was hoping that he would be a shaman like me."

Osbourne frowned. "Your story is strangely similar to mine. I am looking for my mate, Astrid. She, too, was taken by the abominations..." Osbourne's voice trailed off pensively as he remembered what Bodil had said about him not having been the first bear to come to her with such a story. "What is your name?"

"The name I have that is most pronounceable to your kind is Xihhsil."

"Thank you for that." Osbourne smiled. "I am Osbourne. Let us bandage our wounds and rest, and we can continue our pursuit of our foes in the morning. I will take the first watch." The polar bear pulled the bandages from his pack. They seemed meager in comparison to the wounds that he and Xihhsil had suffered, but something was better than nothing.

"Thank you, Osbourne," Xihhsil said.

13

The morning light had barely broken the horizon, its rising corona mottling the sky with bruised shades of red and purple, and Osbourne and Xihhsil had just finished a scant, silent breakfast from what remained of the polar bear's rations.

"Now that I have my strength back," Xihhsil said, "I would like to perform another divination."

"Very well," Osbourne replied. The spell that Bodil had cast upon him was still there, manifesting as a slight, northward tug coming from his core.

Xihhsil closed his eyes and took a deep breath. As he exhaled, he began a weird cadence of hisses and rasps. Osbourne knew it to be an incantation but could understand none of it. The spell continued for a few moments longer, ending when Xihhsil's eyes snapped open.

"Haashan still lives," the naga said incredulously.

"Good," Osbourne replied, "were you able to learn the direction?"

Xihhsil's arm snapped forward, pointing true north. Chills ran down Osbourne's spine. This was not a coincidence.

"Let us get moving," Osbourne said, "We have no time to waste."

"Agreed." Xihhsil nodded.

The polar bear and the naga devoured the ground. Eventually, they could make out a pack of bipedal figures up ahead, and so they slowed to a halt.

"More corrupted beasts," Osbourne said, pulling his axe from his belt.

"Yes…" Xihhsil replied, the word heavy with trepidation.

The two of them came closer, one cautious stride at a time. The bipedal figures, six bears, barely moved. Their armor was dented and cracked, and their bodies bore many open wounds that were crusted with gore, smiles with no eyes. Rashes of rust infected their weapons. And Bodil's spell was pulling Osbourne straight toward them.

Lightning snarled into existence about the head of the polar bear's axe as he called upon his Gift. The corrupted beasts jolted at the sound. Turning, they stalked toward Osbourne and Xihhsil. The naga began to hiss a spell. Golden light ensorcelled his hand, and a bright ray streaked forth as he finished the incantation. It struck the frontmost foe, engulfing the corrupted beast in radiant flames. The abomination collapsed, and the others simply moved around it, uncaring and undeterred. Their lack of remorse for their fallen companion stoked Osbourne's hatred.

He pointed his axe forward. The runes upon the head glowed with greater ardor as a lightning bolt leaped forth, slamming into another foe. Gobbets of rotting flesh exploded through the air as the corrupted beast collapsed. Only four foes remained now, and Osbourne trusted his odds. He charged, his vision already turning red as the rage answered to him.

Xihhsil cast another spell. A second golden ray streaked forth, engulfing another corrupted beast in golden flames as Osbourne closed the distance, his last stride flowing seamlessly into a brutal hack of his axe. One of the corrupted beasts blocked, its shield cracking under the force of the blow. The other two foes swung at Osbourne, one after the other, their weapons whistling as they carved through the air. Osbourne caught the edge of one blade on the rim of his shield, steel snarling against steel; the other blade went low, slicing through the leather covering the polar bear's thigh to bite into the flesh beneath. Osbourne growled in pain as wet warmth spilled out from the wound.

He swung next at the corrupted beast that had wounded him, separating its head from its shoulders with a sickening crack. A ray of light fulgurated past Osbourne's left side, narrowly missing its target. The remaining corrupted beasts surged forward, swiping their weapons at Osbourne. He stepped back into a defensive stance and wove a web of wood and steel that blocked the strikes.

The corrupted beasts struck again. Osbourne raised his shield to block one and rolled with the motion of the blow as he sidestepped the other. A shiver ran down his spine as the abomination's weapon swept past his neck, barely missing it. A moment later, Xihhsil charged, driving his spear forward. One of the corrupted beasts collapsed as the spear punched through its chest. As Xihhsil tore his weapon free, Osbourne swung his axe at the last foe, an etiolated polar bear.

The abomination beat back the blow with its own axe, its eyes now glowing with lurid purple light. "Fools…" the corrupted bear rasped, its throat writhing as it spoke. "Do you not realize the futility of your efforts? We are legion."

Osbourne glared at the polar bear. Whoever was possessing it, was a true foe. "I do not care how many of your minions fall before my axe. I will find Astrid!" Letting out a bloodcurdling roar, the polar bear swung at the corrupted bear, and Xihhsil lunged and thrust his spear.

The corrupted bear blocked Osbourne's axe with its own, the blades grinding against each other as it turned away Xihhsil's spear with its shield.

"You will fall before the might of the Order," the corrupted bear hissed.

The next moments passed in a whirlwind of blades, strikes, blocks, parries, and ripostes; the corrupted bear kept perfect pace with Osbourne and Xihhsil. Until it didn't. Gore sprayed all over Osbourne as Xihhsil skewered the corrupted beast from behind, the tip of his spear sticking out of his foe's chest.

Xihhsil tore his spear free, and a chunk of lead formed in Osbourne's gut as he lowered his axe and gazed at the morbid tableau of their own making. The fight had been easy. Too easy. Osbourne focused inward on Bodil's spell. It had become fainter, weaker. The polar bear's throat went dry. What did that mean for Astrid?

"Are you ready to continue, Osbourne?" Xihhsil said, "There is plenty of time left in the day."

Osbourne glanced up at the sky. It was around noontide. "Aye, that there is. How strong is your guiding spell right now?"

"It has… weakened." Xihhsil frowned.

"I wonder why." Osbourne cocked his head.

As he was about to turn away, metal glinting in the snow caught his eye. He took a step toward it. On the ground, near the corpse of the formerly possessed beast, was a silver chain bearing a golden medallion engraved with an austere panther face, tiny amethysts as its eyes. Osbourne looped his axe on his belt, knelt, and picked up the amulet. It was deathly cold to the touch.

"What did you find?" Xihhsil slithered next to Osbourne.

Osbourne rose and showed the amulet to his companion. "I have seen something like this before."

"Where?" Xihhsil reached out a hand to touch the amulet but stopped. "It has a powerful aura of dark magic about it."

"There was an oracle I stayed with who had an amulet exactly like this on her mantel. She gave me food and rest, and then..." Osbourne's paws tensed. He didn't want to give voice to his next thoughts.

Xihhsil looked again at the amulet, then back at Osbourne. "I have encountered amulets like these before, and they always come in pairs. I can use this one to find the other one. If what you say is true, it is our best chance at finding our loved ones."

"It seems like it is our only chance," Osbourne said, his voice grim. He handed the amulet to Xihhsil. Not so long ago, Osbourne had thought of the naga as mere savages, little better than Bror's *snakes*. No longer.

Xihhsil took the amulet and held it so that the eyes of the tiny panther were level with his own. A sibilant incantation followed. Golden light manifested in the naga's eyes, and the amethyst eyes of the amulet also began glowing. Osbourne reached inward to his own Gift, his muscles tensing as he prepared to unleash a lightning bolt.

Xihhsil's arm trembled as he continued his spell. The glow about the amulet brightened while the light in the naga's eyes flickered, his face tensing into an austere mask of concentration.

Suddenly, radiant, violet sorcery erupted from the amulet as screams of anguish and torment tore through the air. Osbourne and Xihhsil lowered their heads and covered their ears, though the naga maintained his grip on the now-writhing amulet. Osbourne's lightning yearned to be free, the Gift clawing at the restraints upon it as the polar bear's heart pounded. His instincts demanded that he destroy the amulet; it was a blight upon the world.

Osbourne barely held himself back. Xihhsil was still casting his spell. It was the best hope for Astrid.

Another cacophony of shrieking and wailing burst from the amulet, and then it fell still as the purple light about it evanesced in a southward nimbus. The golden light left Xihhsil's eyes while he groaned with exhaustion and let his arms drop.

Osbourne buried his Gift with a deep breath, feeling a measure of relief as his veins stopped burning. "Did it work? Do you know where they are?" Where *she* is, he added silently.

"Yes. The connection between the two amulets is quite strong. It is little wonder that we stopped feeling our spells work. But, I have learned the truth." Xihhsil shuddered as he handed the amulet back to Osbourne. "I saw an Ursidaen crone who dwells in a lone hut to the south. Astrid and Haashan are with her, too, but there is no way to know if they are alive."

"I have been betrayed," Osbourne rumbled as traces of red ringed his vision. "She was never leading me toward Astrid at all. Only to my doom."

"Indeed." Xihhsil frowned. "We have both been deceived."

The red about Osbourne's vision thickened as he gave a long, wordless growl, his mind swirling with thoughts of how he would punish Bodil.

14

The trek was long and grueling. What should have been a full day's travel, at least, was compressed into a few hours as Osbourne and Xihhsil raced against the daylight they had left, stopping for neither food nor water, nearly unliving in their endurance. Now, the hut was within view, barely visible in the rapidly encroaching twilight and further obscured by the shifting humanoid forms in front of it. A pair of lights that looked like guttering torches could also be seen.

Finally, Osbourne and Xihhsil stopped.

Osbourne took a deep breath. His lungs burned, and his heart raced.

"We are expected," Xihhsil said.

"Aye," Osbourne replied, "Of course we are. But, it is of no matter. We must press on."

He was already charging forward, tearing his axe from his belt and unshouldering his shield. His muscles writhed with a vigor born from desperation. With every stride, Osbourne's foes came into clearer focus. There were corrupted bears and gorillas, so many of them, far more than Osbourne had seen in one place before, a tableau of walking decay with an effluvium to match.

Standing prominently among them was a trio of well-muscled panthers, each like an apparition amid the gloom. They wore black armor that was distinguishable from their fur by the purple trim that framed it and golden filigree that gave the hint of an accent. Their paws gripped short staffs that had a svelte, sword-length blade sprouting from each end. The centermost panther pointed at Osbourne and Xihhsil, the cat's eyes turning purple as the herd of corrupted beasts stalked toward the polar bear and the naga.

Osbourne roared, and his vision turned red as electricity surged through his muscles. The runes upon his axe began to glow. Lightning snarled into existence about the blade. Faster and faster, he hurtled forward.

For Astrid.

For Haashan.

For all of the noble warriors who had been condemned to such a horrific fate.

One foe fell, then another; Osbourne swung his axe up and down, to and fro, never slowing, never stopping, sparks bursting with every strike. Xihhsil was not far behind the polar bear, skewering corrupted beasts upon his spear. Still, for all their fury, the two of them struggled to take ground.

Pain wracked Osbourne as a lucky strike sliced into his axe arm. Blood poured from the wound, but Osbourne continued to fight. His axe buried itself deep in the skull of an abomination, sending it to the ground. More pain followed as another corrupted beast struck Osbourne, this time slicing his side, mangling links of his ringmail and punching through the leather beneath.

"More—" Xihhsil was cut off by rasping cries of pain as blades ravaged him.

Osbourne did not turn around; the naga's words barely registered; all he saw was red and black, blood and death, the berserker rage, and the reasons why he needed it. More foes fell amid the never-ending din of cracks and tears.

The panthers loped toward Osbourne, all three sets of eyes phosphorescently purple, all three bladed staffs brandished. Osbourne threw up his head and roared. His skaldic power answered him. New vigor girded his body as he charged the three cats, the lightning about his axe growing louder and brighter as his Gift, too, manifested his wrath. Some of the corrupted beasts dared to bar Osbourne's path, and he butchered them, his vicious axe arcing toward the centermost panther next.

As if the cat had been expecting the move, he turned Osbourne's blow aside with a well-timed sweep of his sword-staff. The other two lunged and thrust their weapons at the polar bear. He threw up his shield and blocked, not yielding a single step, and the panthers wheeled their weapons, sending the lower blades whistling up toward Osbourne. He blocked one blade; the other sliced into his thigh, the wound jetting blood. Osbourne felt the pain only as a dull throb. From his mouth boomed another roar as he cleaved with his axe. Three lightning bolts, crackling with malevolent delight, leaped from the weapon's head, surging toward the panthers. The cats whirled back, but the lightning was faster, smiting their chests and sides and throwing them off guard. Still, they betrayed no signs of pain. That infuriated Osbourne more. For their crimes, he would make sure that these foes knew what pain was before they died.

The berserker was already swinging again, his axe tracing the same arc in the opposite direction, beginning the next storm of blades. And all around, the rest of the corrupted bears and gorillas closed in.

From the depths of Osbourne's crimson rage came a smooth voice that was like steel under a veneer of silk. *Resistance is futile. Ambrose beckons.*

"No!" From on high, Osbourne's axe came down like the wrath of the gods, embedding itself in the centermost panther's skull with a sickening crack, blood gushing out.

The other two panthers moved in to reap their vengeance upon Osbourne as the corrupted beasts struck. From behind streaked a golden ray, then another; each one felled a foe. Osbourne barely noticed, focused only on the carnage directly ahead. For every wound he inflicted, he received one in return, red lines appearing all over him as though he were a gruesome canvas. Blood, so much blood, poured out of him.

Desperation powered Osbourne's next blows. His shield beat back a corrupted beast before cannoning into the face of one of the panthers, caving it in with a wet crack. The only sound that would have been sweeter was Astrid's voice. The dead panther unceremoniously collapsed as a third golden ray cut down another corrupted beast.

And the third panther ran away, soon melding with the darkness beyond. Osbourne roared, raging against the display of cowardice, and he vented it on the remaining foes until there were none left, only corpses.

Lucidity fell upon Osbourne like a lead curtain, dropping him to his knees. His flesh throbbed with agony, and his bones were like rubber. His wounds continued to weep blood. The lightning about his axe went out.

Still, his task was not done. Osbourne forced himself to rise. He might as well have been trying to lift Tordok's axe. A groan slid out of his mouth as he was finally back on his hind paws. Glancing over at Xihhsil, Osbourne frowned when he saw that the naga was not moving. He wanted to check on his companion but knew that he did not have the energy to spare, not when he could barely keep himself standing.

"Mother Fjardi, preserve him," Osbourne whispered before staggering to the hut where he had taken refuge not so long ago.

15

The hut's door was open, and no fire burned within. Osbourne entered. As he crossed the threshold, he drew up the minute portion of his Gift that was still available to him. A tendril of lightning, hissing, and guttering, manifested about the upper part of his axe's blade, providing precious little light by which to see. The table, chairs, and bed were overturned, forming a loose circle around a wooden hatch with a stout iron handle.

Shame formed a hard knot in Osbourne's chest. How had he missed something that was now so obvious? It would have been so easy. Astrid had been right there the whole time.

Osbourne took a deep breath, wincing with pain as he inhaled and wincing again as he exhaled. He was here now. That was what mattered. The polar bear walked toward the hatch, his axe readied. Once there, he pulled on the handle. Both he and the hatch groaned as the hinges yielded, revealing a descending stone stairwell. He took another deep breath. This was it. This was where he would be reunited with Astrid.

The polar bear descended, one ponderous step after another. As the stairwell flattened out, it opened into a room of bare earth that was as large as the dwelling above. Upon the floor lay a single black bear: Bodil. Next to her lay Astrid's shield, the replaced planks still unpainted.

"No..." Osbourne's jaw dropped as a maelstrom of bewilderment and anger reared up within him. "No..." She was supposed to be here. She had to be here.

Osbourne stepped toward Bodil, raising his axe. The black bear was now clad in black robes with purple trim, and she wore the amulet with the golden panther face, the twin to the one Osbourne carried. And she was stirring.

Forcing his emotions down, Osbourne knelt next to Bodil, holding his ersatz torch over her. She groaned.

"So," Osbourne said as neutrally as he could manage, "you are still alive."

A wan grin formed on Bodil's face as she opened her eyes to meet Osbourne's gaze. "And you... You are too late, much too late indeed."

"Why?" Osbourne tightened his grip on his axe. "Tell me everything."

"Can you not already see?" Bodil managed a weak, cough-riddled laugh, and blood started trickling from her nose. "Astrid is already gone."

"By your paw, no doubt," Osbourne growled. It was all too clear to him that Bodil had delved deep into her Gift recently. That was why she was so close to death without bearing any battle wounds. "Why did you do this?"

"For the Order..." Bodil's smile widened ever so slightly. "To set things right..."

"Set things right?" Osbourne's voice reared up such that he was nearly roaring. He was sorely tempted to end Bodil's life right then and there. "How are packs of beasts infected with dark magic anything close to right? That is the taint of the goddess of death, and you will pay the price for trafficking with her."

"You have so much might within you, Osbourne." Another etiolated laugh left Bodil's mouth. "Berserker, skald, heir to your father's Gift... And yet, you know so little, so very little indeed."

"My patience wears thin."

"So does my life. Tell me, Osbourne: which do you think will run out first?"

"Tell me where Astrid is. Now."

Bodil shrugged half-heartedly. "She is already well beyond my paws, and certainly beyond yours."

"You lie!"

"What reason have I to lie? I am nearly dead, and you will never see your mate again. The Order will see to that. They will help her ascend as she was meant to."

"Ascend?" Osbourne growled, "Order? Explain yourself. Now."

"The Order of Ambrose, of course, the servants of Sod's true god, who will reward..." The last words left Bodil's mouth with a sibilant wheeze, and then she fell still.

Osbourne threw up his head and roared. He roared, and he roared, and he roared. When he was finally done, his gaze fell upon Astrid's shield, and he took it gently, lovingly. Even now, he could envision her blue eyes gleaming in the daylight, beckoning him. Everything had gone by so fast, it seemed. They had been best friends as cubs, playing pretend battles in pretend lands, and then they had fallen in love through trysts under the three moons, and now...

"Do not mourn for me, Osbourne." The voice, so warm and reassuring, could only belong to Astrid.

But, it wasn't real. How could it be? Osbourne closed his eyes and shook his head. Astrid was gone. Osbourne was the only one in the cellar.

The polar bear thought that he had opened his eyes again, but he instead saw the light, so much light, all rising northward as Sha-Jara, the world trees, blessed Terran with another day. The polar bear stood in a verdant sward with a thick, ancient oak as its silent sentinel. Osbourne recognized the tree like the back of his paw; there was no counting how many times he and Astrid had met beneath its branches.

"Why am I here?" Osbourne's gaze darted around. "I do not understand..."

A white, almost spectral, form appeared at the edge of the sward, walking toward Osbourne. His jaw dropped as he realized that the newcomer was another polar bear. Astrid. She wore a white gown trimmed in floral patterns the same color as her eyes, the same gown she had worn on their wedding day.

"My love," Osbourne whispered.

Smiling, Astrid closed the distance to her mate. "Yes, Ozzy." She laid a paw on his cheek. "It is me."

"But how? Why?"

Melancholy wilted Astrid's smile. "I wish I could tell you, but my time is already short. You do not need to find me, Osbourne. I will come back to you. I promise."

"I need you with me now." Osbourne lurched forward and pulled Astrid into his embrace. "Please, do not leave."

For a moment, warmth permeated Osbourne. Then, it was gone, replaced by intense, slicing cold. Astrid turned paler with each passing moment until she started crumbling to ashes, her eyes black and devoid of life.

"No!" Osbourne wailed, clutching Astrid tighter.

It was no use. Speck by speck, piece by piece, she drifted away.

And then, Osbourne was back in the hut.

"I will find you, my love," Osbourne whispered, tears trailing down his face. "Nothing will keep us apart." Astrid's shield in his paw, Osbourne rose and went back up the stairwell, leaving the hut. He still had one more task before his work here was done.

The polar bear found Xihhsil again, still lying motionless in the snow. Osbourne checked for a pulse and found none. More tears fell from his eyes. The naga, like Osbourne, had been searching for a loved one. And now, both were dead.

Willing the lightning about his axe to unravel, Osbourne put the weapon back on his belt, picked up Xihhsil's body, and carried it to the hut. He then did the same for all of the corrupted corpses that were still intact. They had once been proud warriors of Ursidaen and Primean and deserved to be treated as such now. Osbourne's whole body burned from the exertion of the grim work, but it was not done, not yet.

Now standing outside the hut, Osbourne pulled his axe from his belt, raised it to the sky, and cried, "Mighty Tordok, I send these valorous warriors to your realm!" The polar bear's Gift surged through him, and a lightning bolt fulminated from his axe and struck the hut, setting it ablaze.

Higher and higher the flames went, turning night into day as they speared up toward the purple-black sky.

And Osbourne stood.

And Osbourne watched.

Glossary

Akksardi- Akksardi is the Ursidaen god of wisdom, knowledge, and justice. However, he is sometimes worshipped as a god of war in conjunction with Tordok. Akksardi is the leader of the Ursidaen pantheon and is married to Fjardi. Most of the time, Akksardi appears as a thoroughly aged black bear with only his right eye, and he is often depicted wearing a gray robe and hat while holding his spear. However, it is known that he is a shapeshifter. His holy symbol is a scroll, and his colors are white and blue.

Aldmist- This swamp nation is home to Sod's enigmatic lizards.

Clan Eldingblod- One of the many clans of Ursidaen, Clan Eldingblod lives in the southeastern region of their country. Their name translates to "Lightning Blood," and their main symbol is a bear paw gripping a lightning bolt.

Fjardi- Fjardi is the Ursidaen goddess of life, fertility, maternity, and rejuvenation. She appears as a large grizzly bear with light, chestnut brown fur. She bears a warm, motherly expression and wears a vibrant green dress with multi-hued lace. Due to the fact that she is the wife of Akksardi, she is one of the more widely worshiped deities among the Ursidaens, and they often refer to her as Mother Fjardi. Her holy symbol is a bear paw holding a cornucopia, and her colors are forest green and chestnut brown.

Hafna- An Ursidaen military unit consisting of three hundred warriors. The Hafna is the basic unit of organization from which smaller packs and warbands are drawn according to the needs of the mission and the interpersonal relationships of the bears.

Havaeborg- This is one of the major towns of Clan Eldingblod, and it is the hometown of the bear pack sent to investigate the rumors of Primean encroachment.

Kraan- Affectionately known as Grandfather Kraan, he is the Ursidaen deity of fire, heat, hearth, and light. He is a jolly old grizzly bear and is quite large even for an Ursidaen. He mostly wears simple, comfortable clothes while his teeth grip a wooden pipe from which smoke eternally trails. His main role is watching over Ursidaen homes: he is the fire in the hearth that provides heat to cook their meals and light to guide them back home after a long day of labor. He also watches over the children. His colors are brown and orange, and his holy symbol is his wooden pipe.

Lake Skalinnsjo- This lake is located in the south/southeastern region of Ursidaen. It is a landmark to show that one is approaching Aldmist, and naga are known to live here.

Naga- Aquatic, snake-like humanoids who live in tribes along the borders of Aldmist, Primean, and Ursidaen with no nation to call their own. The naga tribes skirmish amongst themselves and with all three of their larger neighbors.

Odofrélsa- This is the title of higher-ranking warriors in the ancient language of Ursidaen who are neither Usyling nor Trynjul. However, their lack of magical and supernormal powers often means that Odofrélsa are accorded more respect because they must survive with their blade, their wits, and their companions. As such, Odofrélsa are often picked for leadership positions in Ursidaen's military, but they will sometimes form more specialized, irregular units.

Odolig- This is the title of the warrior rank in the ancient language of Ursidaen. The Odolig are the backbone of Ursidaen's military and culture. Every cub is trained in the way of the warrior from birth, and completing the trials to earn this title is also the rite of passage into adulthood. As such, unless otherwise stated, every adult Ursidaen is considered an Odolig.

Order of Ambrose- This organization is sometimes referred to simply as, "The Order." It is an emerging power on Sod of shadowy origins. The Order of Ambrose recruits beasts of all stripes into its fold, and it will do absolutely everything to achieve its fanatical goals. Their calling cards are panther imagery and the colors black and purple.

Primean- This is the nation of gorillas on Sod, and the gorillas themselves are known as Primeans.

Skald- This is the title of the warrior-bards (or warrior-poets) of Ursidaen. These bears learn the legends and lore of their homeland, which results in the manifestation of a special kind of magic that a beast doesn't have to be born with. Skalds use this magic to grant vigor and inspiration to their fellow beasts. Skalds are higher ranking than Odolig, but not as high ranking as Trynjul or Usyling.

The Gift- This is the catch-all term to describe the inborn magical powers of any beast on Sod. Common forms of the Gift include elemental conjuration and manipulation, as well as divination. But, the Gift is by no means limited to these, and the intensity with which it manifests also varies.

The Heartlands- This is Sod's central region from which the lions rule much of the rest of the continent.

Tordok- Tordok is the Ursidaen god of storms and war. He is a mighty grizzly bear who wears a breastplate over his leathers, and he wields an axe named Svarnar that was forged by Akksardi himself. It is with this axe that Tordok channels his power over wind, lightning, and thunder, often conducting storms as if they were an orchestra. He is the son of Akksardi and Fjardi. His holy symbol is a bear paw gripping a lightning bolt while his colors are gray and blue.

Trynjul- This is the title of the warrior-mage rank in the ancient language of Ursidaen. Trynjul are higher ranking than Odolig and receive more training, though they must complete another set of trials as well. However, their ability to combine sorcerous powers with superlative bladework often results in devastating results. As such, the Trynjul form the specialized portions of Ursidaen's military.

Ursidaen- This is the nation of bears on Sod, and the bears themselves are also known as Ursidaens.

Usyling- This is the title of the berserker rank in the ancient language of Ursidaen. Though Usyling is a higher rank than Odolig and requires an additional set of trials, the berserker rage itself is inborn and typically reveals itself around the time of puberty.

About the Author

Isaiah Burt is a fantasy author who has been telling stories since he was old enough to hold a crayon and likes to think that moving up to a pen has helped him. He considers Elric of Melniboné, the Death Gate Cycle, and Planescape to be his biggest influences, with Bionicle being a significant honorable mention. Along with writing, he also is an avid player of both Dungeons & Dragons and Warhammer, and he has a rather large Magic: The Gathering collection. He lives with his wife in their cave of wonders in Washington, USA.

His blog contains more of his stories and a list of his published works. It can be found here:
https://talesofvalorandwoe.wixsite.com/zeragabaalkhal

Find him on Facebook here:
https://www.facebook.com/IsaiahBurtAuthor

Should a soul feel generous enough, one might send him a donation here:
https://ko-fi.com/zeragabaalkhal

Made in the USA
Columbia, SC
18 November 2024